FUGITIVE OF MAGIC

DRAGON'S GIFT THE PROTECTOR BOOK 1

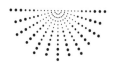

LINSEY HALL

To Ora and Richard Callaway, the loveliest people.

ACKNOWLEDGMENTS

Thank you, Ben, for everything. There would be no books without you.

Thank you to Lindsey Loucks for your excellent editing. The book is immensely better because of you! Thank you to Crystal Jeffs, for your help making the story better. Thank you to Jessi Crosby, for your keen eye. Thank you to Jesse Ammons for your help with selecting Nix's cars. Couldn't have done it without you!

The Dragon's Gift series is a product of my two lives: one as an archaeologist and one as a novelist. Combining these two took a bit of work. I'd like to thank my friends, Wayne Lusardi, the State Maritime Archaeologist for Michigan, and Douglas Inglis and Veronica Morris, both archaeologists for Interactive Heritage, for their ideas about how to have a treasure hunter heroine that doesn't conflict too much with archaeology's ethics. The Author's Note contains a bit more about this if you are interested.

CHAPTER ONE

It was business as usual until about five o'clock. That's when the demons showed up.

Five of them crossed the street toward my shop like they owned the whole damned road. The late-winter sun set behind them, making their forms blaze in orange light. Through the wide glass window, it was easy to see their bulging muscles, prominent horns, and the weapons that hung off their utility vests.

"Hey, Nix, you thinking what I'm thinking?" asked my friend Cass, who helped me run our magical treasure-hunting business.

"Yeah. They look like violently decorated Christmas trees."

Cass laughed, her red hair gleaming in the light.

"Ridiculous," I said. "Everyone knows you only needed one good weapon at a time."

"You think they know how to use all those things?" she asked.

"Not as well as we do." I grinned. "I've been hankering for a good fight. What do you say we meet them outside?"

"Good plan, Batman." She glanced around at the enchanted artifacts on the shelves. "Be a shame to lose any stock."

"Exactly."

I stepped out from behind the shop counter. We strode toward the glass door, passing by shelves stuffed to the brim with the fruits of our treasure-hunting labors. We risked life and limb to recover these artifacts from enchanted tombs and temples. Though the ones now on our shelves were replicas, they were each enchanted with a spell. I wasn't about to let some demons steal from us.

As the demons reached the sidewalk, I pulled open the door, then leaned against the jam.

The five of them were massive—each at least six and a half feet tall. All possessed power—dark magic from the rank smell of it.

Good. I liked a challenge. And my boots hadn't kicked much ass in the last couple weeks. They were getting bored, and I was convinced that demon blood conditioned the leather nicely.

"Can I help you, gentlemen?" I raised a brow, pointedly eyeing their horns. Demons weren't allowed to walk freely on Earth. Too violent and conspicuous. Humans weren't supposed to know about magic, and demons would blow our cover.

The biggest demon stepped forward and spoke, his voice a growl. "Here to make a purchase."

"Mm-hm, sure, yeah." I nodded, glancing down at his weapons. "You usually come dressed for a fight when doing a little shopping? And with four buddies?"

Maybe they were out for a boys' night of antique shopping, but I doubted it. They'd showed up at the end of business hours, dressed to kill.

Literally.

Since we had a robbery attempt a least once a week and the last one had been ten days ago, we were due.

"How about you forget about stealing from us so that I don't have to get your blood on my clothes?" I really loved this vampire Hello Kitty T-shirt, and demon blood was a bitch to get out of fabric. Good for leather, bad for cotton.

The demon didn't answer. Instead, the rank scent of his magic flared, like a garbage fire blazing bright. It was all the warning I got. All the warning I needed.

I called upon my magic, what little I had. It shivered through me, down my arm and towards my hand as I envisioned a conjuring shield that would block whatever magic he chose to throw at me. I didn't have the badass violent kind of power that Cass did, but my conjuring came in handy in fights.

But instead of creating a fireball or some other magical weapon, the demon shoved his magical signature away and reached for the blade at his hip. My silver shield appeared on my arm just as he drew the long knife and swung at me.

It clanged off my shield, making my arm vibrate.

Beside me, Cass hurled a fireball at the demon standing next to my attacker. The ball of flame raced through the air and crashed into his chest, blasting him backward. She turned her attention to another demon.

My demon attacker raised his blade again, clearly determined to plow through my shield this time. As he brought it down, I conjured a knife and plunged it into his side, dodging his blade that hurtled toward my shoulder. It sliced through the fabric of my shirt, but only left a thin cut in my flesh. Pain flared briefly, but I used it as fuel.

I kneed the demon in the crotch and yanked my blade out of his side, then stabbed it into his chest and twisted.

He grunted, his eyes going wide.

"Go back to hell." I kicked him in the chest, sending him flying backward.

Behind me, a demon tried to creep past, sneaking into the shop. I spun, swinging my shield like I'd seen Captain America do in a movie, and nailed him in the back of the head.

Thanks, 'Cap.

The shield clanged loudly, as if he had a skull made of iron, and he wobbled. I plunged my blade into his back, right where I guessed his heart would be. Sometimes it was hard to tell with demons.

From the way he sagged, I must have hit my mark.

I withdrew the blade and let him fall.

We had this in the bag.

I turned to see how Cass was making out with the fifth and final demon. Probably wiping the floor with them, if I knew her.

She'd downed the fourth demon with a fireball. His crispy remains sat on the sidewalk like a burned turkey dinner. But the fifth was shimmering with some kind of magic that smelled like a swamp and prickled against my skin. All magic had a signature—scent, taste, feel—and whatever this guy was about to do, it was big.

Ah, hell.

I raised my blade to throw it at him, but before it left my fingertips, he'd split into two different demons. Both were identical.

Double hell.

That was some rare, dangerous magic.

The demon split again, making three. And again.

Well, this was going poorly.

I hurled my knife at the main demon, but he dived behind a car just in time. The blade whizzed past him. I turned my attention to the demon who charged me, conjuring another dagger.

"Please be an illusion," I muttered as I threw my knife at him. It plunged into his broad chest and he grunted, stumbling back.

Damn it.

"They're real." Cass threw a fireball at one. It crashed against his chest in a flash of sparks, throwing him backward into a light post behind.

"A Multiplicita." I was too close for a bow and arrow, my preferred weapon, so I conjured a sword. In a world of magic, conjuring wasn't that exciting.

Unless you could conjure pointy things and knew how to use them.

Which I did.

Unfortunately, there were now a *lot* of demons. They kept appearing, one by one, from behind the car where the host demon hid.

Cass could light the vehicle up with a massive fireball, but the damned thing belonged to an Order of the Magica member. Government officials did not like it when you destroyed their property, and we *really* didn't want to get on their bad side.

The demons chose that moment to charge. I dodged the first, swiping out with my blade as he passed. It sliced through his side and he shouted, but kept stumbling for the shop. The next was on me almost immediately. I plunged my blade into his gut and side-stepped.

At my side, Cass took down two demons with the same fireball. Two more charged her.

I pressed my fingertips to the comms charm at my neck, igniting its magic. "Del! We need backup!"

"At the shop?" Del's voice crackled through the comms charm. She was our best friend and the third leg of this operation.

"Yeah." I swung my blade at a demon who tried to dodge past me, swiping the steel across his neck. Blood spurted, splashing against my face. Warm and wet and gross.

Through the glass door, I could see the demon who'd gotten past me ransacking the shelves.

Whatever they were after, there was no way in hell I'd let them have it.

Cass took out another demon with one of her handy fireballs. The smell of burning demon flesh made bile rise in my throat. Contrary to popular thought, it did not smell like grilled chicken. This was getting out of hand. Keeping a low profile was our safety blanket. And this was not low profile.

Down the street, Del burst out of the door that led up to our apartments. She raced toward us, sword drawn and her black hair flying behind her. Thank fates we lived in a magical town or this shit would be even more conspicuous.

"Behind the car!" Cass shouted.

Del veered right, no doubt to search for the host demon who was creating our attackers.

I turned my attention back to the shop. The demon inside had found whatever he was looking for, because he now charged the door, something lumpy tucked under his arm.

I stepped into his path and raised my sword. "Dream on, buddy."

As if I'd let him get away.

A hard arm wrapped around my middle and swung me away from the door, hurling me hard against a lamp post. Pain flared in my shoulder, blurring my vision. My blade dropped from my limp hand and I collapsed.

Crap.

I scrambled to my feet as my new attacker bore down on me. He was a demon like the rest, tall and broad and armed like a mercenary out to take down a zombie baseball team. The weapons hanging from his vest clanged against each in a violent chorus.

Of all his weapons, he'd chosen a massive curved sword. He raised it overhead, his gaze burning down at me, and swung.

My heart thundered in my ears as I dived, scooping up my blade and narrowly avoiding getting cleaved in two. His blade banged against the ground. I swiped out with my own sword, going low and for the legs like I favored. They never saw that coming.

This guy didn't, either, and he toppled like a tree, crashing to the sidewalk.

Behind me, Cass and Del were taking care of the rest of the demons. Del wielded her sword like a tornado of death while Cass hurled fireballs at the few surviving demons.

Ahead, my prey was sprinting down the sidewalk, past the old brick buildings that made up Factory Row. He was twenty feet away, two of his buddies at his side.

I left my sword on the sidewalk since it would do me no good in a footrace.

"Watch the shop!" I sprinted after them, leaping over a flock of pigeons that decided to land on the sidewalk in front of me. I called upon my magic, letting it shiver through me, and conjured a bow and arrow.

I was about to fire when a crowd of revelers poured out of Potions & Pastilles, our favorite coffee shop, spilling onto the sidewalk in front of me.

Shit.

I didn't have a clear shot. There were six brain-dead partiers blocking me from my quarry.

I pushed through the crowd, breaking out to see the three demons stopped at the crosswalk as a bus trundled in front of them. Factory Row, where we lived and worked, was usually quiet. Not today.

I drew back the string on my bow and fired. Satisfaction warmed my chest as the arrow sped toward the closest demon and hit him in the back. He stumbled to his knees.

A shout sounded from behind me, a deep bark. I glanced back. Through the crowd of revelers, who now scattered at the sight of my bow, another demon raced toward us. He stopped dead still and hurled something high into the air.

It was a tiny black pebble.

Ah, hell.

I turned back to the demon I was pursuing, sprinting toward him as I watched him snag the little back pebble out of the air. He threw it onto the ground in front of him. It exploded in a cloud of silvery dust.

Shit, shit, shit.

A transportation charm.

The two demons leapt inside the dust, disappearing to who the hell knew where.

Generally speaking, it was a piss-poor idea to follow demons into unknown portals.

But no one *ever* stole from me. It fucked with my track record.

Chucking good sense in favor of victory, I sprinted for the cloud of dust that was now dissipating. The portal would be gone any second. I said a quick prayer to the fates and hurtled into it.

～

My next step carried me into darkness.

What the hell? It had been dusk on the other side of the portal. But this was *dark.*

I blinked to regain my vision. We were in an alley. It was vaguely familiar, but something was seriously off. Ahead of me, the demons sprinted away. They ran single file, with my target in the lead, protected by the demon behind him.

I raised my bow, aimed, and fired. The arrow whizzed through the air, striking the last demon in the back. He stumbled and fell, leaving my prey exposed. He seemed to realize that, however, and dodged left, hiding behind a dumpster.

His magic swelled briefly, a strange signature that I'd never felt before. It rumbled in my chest, as if a jet plane had landed nearby. It turned my insides to jello and made my knees tremble.

Depending on the strength of their magic, supernaturals gave off different strength signatures. And this guy was *strong.*

Scary, piss-your-pants strong.

What the hell kind of magic was this? And why hadn't he used it back at the shop?

Dread opened a dark hole in my chest. Wherever we were—in this strange shadow land—he was comfortable using his creepy dark magic.

The ground rumbled beneath my feet, trembling like an

earthquake was about to tear through the earth. Ahead of me, the paved alley split open, a chasm opening up in the ground.

Well, fuck.

I was cut off from the demon, who was on the other side of the alley, hiding behind the dumpster. The crack raced in front of me, cutting me off.

I sucked in a breath as my heart pounded in my ears, then took a running jump over the crevasse. I made it to the other side, but teetered on the edge, arms wheeling.

The breath whooshed out of my body as I envisioned falling into the deep dark pit behind me.

Barely, I managed to right myself, then sprinted toward the brick wall at the edge of the alley, running alongside the building as the crack in the middle of the passage creaked and groaned, widening. I had to kill this demon or I'd be swallowed into the earth.

Along with this entire creepy alley.

When I reached the dumpster, I swung my bow over my back so that it hung with the string crossed over my chest, and hauled myself up onto the lid of the dumpster. I was past sneakiness now—totally out of time for that—and I thundered across the lid. I reached for an arrow in the sheath at my back and dropped down onto the demon who crouched against the side.

His wide eyes met mine.

I stabbed him in the neck with the arrow. "Didn't expect to see me, did you?"

His mouth opened and blood gurgled out of the corner of his lips. Something heavy rammed into my side and pain flared, an agony that definitely spelled *cracked ribs.*

I glanced down to see the demon's fist balled at his side.

The damned demon had punched me!

I shoved the arrow deeper into his neck. The strength that had fueled him finally faded, and he collapsed against the wall. The life drifted out of him.

I grabbed the lumpy package from under the demon's arm and scrambled away from him. In a few moments, his body would disappear back to whatever Underworld he'd come from.

That was the thing about killing demons while on Earth— they didn't really die. They just went back to the Underworld and got another go. Like a video game.

It was why I didn't have to feel guilty when I killed one.

At least he hadn't gotten what he'd come for.

I was about to peek into the package to see which enchanted object he'd stolen when a noise sounded from down the alley. A moment later, magic flared.

This signature was entirely different—it felt like a cool breeze blowing inside my mind, then burned like fire.

I winced, looking up and squinting into the darkness. The demon's earth-breaking magic hadn't extended up that way, so the alley looked normal, though very creepy. A dark mist had started to flow over the ground as the magical signature filled the air.

Whatever was happening down the alley, it was dangerous. Dark magic. The illegal kind that hurt as well as helped.

I needed to get the hell out of here—wherever here was.

Shit. I didn't know where I was, nor did I have a transport charm or the ability to teleport.

Quietly, I stood, keeping the package tucked tightly under my arm. I was about to turn and head back the way I'd come when a small flash of white caught my eye.

Hair. White hair. And a dark cloak.

There were two figures grappling down the alley, as if they'd spilled out of a smaller street into this one.

Not my business.

But as I turned to go, I got a better glimpse of the white-haired figure.

It was an old man.

The bigger figure was attacking an old man.

That was screwed up.

Fights were common in Magic's Bend—if we were still even in my town—but I wasn't down with people attacking old folks.

I sprinted toward them, the package tucked under my arm. I opened my mouth to shout, but a silver light burst from the pair.

The flash blinded me and I stumbled, nearly losing my hard-won prize. Blinded, I righted myself, my vision clearing just in time to see the larger figure running away. I couldn't make out a thing about him—I didn't even know if he was a man or a woman.

The old man was on the ground, lying on the cobblestones in a way that made dread rise like dark tar inside my chest.

Shit.

I sprinted faster, lungs burning, and fell to my knees at his side. His black cloak spread over the cobblestones, and his white hair was stark in the dim light. His eyes were closed and mouth partially opened.

A silvery-white blade protruded from his chest, red blood welling around it.

"Shit, shit." I set aside my package and patted the man's cheek. "Come on, guy."

But his eyes didn't open.

Panic beat like bird's wings inside my chest. "Come on, you gotta wake up. You'll be fine."

He didn't move. Stillness shrouded him.

I pressed my fingertips to my comms charm, heart pounding. "Cass? Del? I need backup. A man is dying."

No sound crackled from the charm, and its magic lay dormant.

Shit.

Screw it.

My gaze raced over the old man as I conjured a thick white towel. I had *no* idea what to do—I preferred action movies over medical dramas—but I was alone in this alley and this dude was dying.

Carefully, I slipped the blade from his chest and pressed the towel to the wound.

"Come on."

But he didn't move. He was dying. He was some kind of Magica—a magic user—not a shifter or demon or fae or anything like that. His magic fluttered inside of him, as if desperate to be free of his dying body.

The magic that I hid deep inside myself screamed at me to steal his power. I was a Conjurer, yes. But I had more magic than that.

Much more.

The only problem was that it was a dangerous, forbidden magic.

FireSoul magic. The reason the Order of the Magica hunted us like dogs. There were a few Magica who were also FireSouls—and we were reviled.

Like my friends Cass and Del, I could steal this man's unique magical gift for my own. The process required that he die, but that was a given, now. His blood was soaking through the towel I pressed to the wound.

My heart thundered and tears pricked my eyes as the FireSoul inside me screamed to tear out his magic. Possess it.

But hot on its heels, bile rose in my throat. I *couldn't*. Not only was it illegal—just being caught as a FireSoul would get me life in prison—the mere idea made cold sweat break out on my body.

I didn't know why I'd always had this strong aversion to stealing powers—neither Cass nor Del had this problem—but it overwhelmed me. Neither of them liked stealing magic, but even the idea of it made me physically ill. There was something in my mind—in my past—that was weird and dark as hell, but I had no idea what.

I sucked in ragged breaths, trying to get ahold of myself as I staunched the blood from his wound. I hadn't had an attack like this in a long time. One—I hadn't wanted to steal a power in a long time. And two—I hadn't had a full-on freak out of this magnitude.

But I sure as heck wouldn't be stealing from some old man. From what I knew, a FireSoul had to kill their victim. Apparently, not me.

Think, think.

But there was no thinking my way out of this. I had to fight my urge to steal his magic as I tried to save his life.

"Come on, guy," I whispered. "You have to wake up."

He lay still, the flesh of his face sagging.

Tears burned at my eyes, which was stupid. I didn't even know this guy. No reason to cry over him. There was even a chance that he was a jerk. Maybe *he'd* been attacking the other guy and had lost.

Nah.

That was dumb. This was just a damned tragedy, and I knew it.

My shoulders sagged. The towel was soaked through with blood, and the man lay still and quiet.

His magic drifted away as the life left him. My FireSoul hunger died along with him. An iron band tightened around my heart.

This hurt a hell of a lot more than I'd expected. Maybe because I'd always had a soft spot for old folks. I had no memories before the age of fifteen, but I figured that maybe I'd been raised by grandparents or something.

I shook away the sad thoughts.

This dude was *not* my grandfather. If I even had one.

And I was sitting over his body in a sketchy part of town, like a kid with their hand in a cookie jar of murder. I could not get caught for this. No way. That'd lead to questions, and questions would lead to trouble.

I took one last look at the guy. He looked quiet. Peaceful. It was the best I was going to get in this situation.

My limbs were heavy as I stood. Since I didn't want to leave anything at the scene, I conjured a dark plastic bag and stuck the towel inside it, then used the edge of my vampire kitty shirt to wipe my fingerprints off the weird white blade.

Hopefully that did the trick.

Quickly, I stooped and grabbed my package, then took off down the street, headed for the entrance to the alley. As I walked, I conjured a damp towel, wiping the demon blood from my face and getting the worst of it off my clothes. I stashed the dirty towel in the bag and hoped I wouldn't draw stares when I got to the street.

Down this way, the ground was still split, but fortunately, no one lived at this end of the alley. Hopefully no one had seen me.

I ran as far from the edge of the crevasse as I could. In the dark, I couldn't even see down to the bottom.

At the end of the alley, I sprinted out onto a main road, then pulled up short and pressed myself back against the building so I didn't get hit by a car. The sky had brightened as soon as I got out of the alley. Though the sun had set, it was still gleaming, and there was more than enough light to brighten the sky.

Weird.

I turned back to the alley, where it had been dark as midnight. *What the hell?*

It wasn't dark any longer. Just a bit dim, like the rest of the street. And the deep crevasse in the ground was gone.

That had *definitely* been real. So where the hell had it gone?

"This is freaking weird," I muttered.

"Eh?" an old woman poked her head out of the window next to where I stood, her dark eyes meeting mine.

I nearly jumped out of my skin. "Holy crap."

"Don't take crap's name in vain." She cackled, her two chins wobbling joyfully.

"Uh…" I glanced around, realizing that I was near Darklane, the part of Magic's Bend where dark magic practitioners lived. Dark magic wasn't necessarily evil, but it certainly walked the line. It was the kind of magic that harmed as well as helped. But that didn't make it bad, necessarily. Like blood magic—illegal if you did it without the consent of the donor, but otherwise acceptable.

While a lot of these supernaturals were occasionally on the wrong side of the law, they weren't outright lawbreakers. The Order of the Magica would crack down on that. They were just rather…eclectic.

"Would you like some crow's foot stew, dearie?" the woman asked.

Eclectic like this lady.

"Uh, no thanks. Pizza is really more my game." I nodded my thanks and stepped away from the wall. "You have a good day, ma'am."

I backed away from her, but her eyes narrowed as they inspected me. "You look like you're out to cause trouble, with your kitty shirt and your butt-kicking boots. And those jeans. You really ought to mend them."

I glanced down at my torn jeans and heavy black boots.

"I'll get right on that," I muttered.

Not. I liked my torn jeans and kick-ass boots, along with my cartoon T-shirts. Not only were the shirts funny, but demons and dudes were usually stupid. They never thought that a girl in a kitty shirt would conjure a bat and beat your brains in before you could blink.

In fairness, I only did that if they caused trouble. Like the demons who'd stolen from me. One of whom was now dead in that alley, along with an unknown old man.

I took one last glance at the alley, searching for a street sign.

Fair Fortune Alley.

Sure. I almost chuckled, but the thought of the dead man stopped me. Too real.

"See ya later." I saluted the old woman and turned, then ran.

But it didn't matter how far down the street I got. Something was going to chase me. I just knew it.

CHAPTER TWO

I had to ditch the bag of bloody towels a few streets down before I could hail a cab. I wasn't usually a big fan of cabs, but I was too far from home to hoof it.

The cab that pulled to a stop was painted a glittery purple, and the seats were pink leather.

"Nice ride." I climbed into the back seat, slipping my bow and quiver off my back. Though I could conjure things, I couldn't make them disappear. I could sell them, but most mages could tell that the object was conjured and not original. For some reason, they didn't like that.

"Thanks." A pixie with green hair turned and grinned at me. She was pretty and about my age. "Where to, beautiful?"

"Factory Row. Potions & Pastilles." Out of habit, I didn't give the name of my shop, Ancient Magic. Though it was legally above board, I was so used to lying low that it was natural to not mention my true destination.

"Sure thing." The pixie pulled away from the curb.

I must have gotten most of the demon blood off me, or the cabbie never would have picked me up. I slouched in my seat, wearily eyeing the street outside. My ribs sang with pain, every breath sending a sharp knife stab through me.

The car zipped through the historic district, which was full of beautiful old buildings from the early eighteenth century, when Magic's Bend had first been settled by supernaturals.

It was a weeknight, but foot traffic still clogged the sidewalks as people headed to the bars and restaurants that filled this part of town. Though almost everyone looked human, I spotted a few shifters in their animal form and one massive woman who glowed with a bright yellow light. Though many supernaturals went out amongst humans—and even lived amongst them—non-human looking supernaturals were required by law to stay in wholly magical cities like Magic's Bend.

Cass, Del, and I didn't come down here often, preferring to stick to Factory Row. It was full of outcasts and weirdos, and that suited us.

The business district flashed by next. The tall glass buildings gleamed with light. Magic's Bend was the largest supernatural city in the world—fully operational with its own airport, hospital, museums. All that good stuff.

By the time we turned onto factory row, full dark had fallen. The tall old buildings were as familiar as my own face in the mirror. We lived and worked in the recently revitalized factory district. The old brick buildings from the nineteenth and early twentieth centuries had been refurbished and turned into shops and apartments.

The cab pulled to a halt in front of Potions & Pastilles. The warm light glowed from the windows of the coffee shop/bar, illuminating the crowd that had gathered for the craft beer and whiskey that my friends Connor and Claire specialized in.

"We're here!" The pixie grinned back at me, her teeth so bright and white they almost blinded me.

"Thanks." I dug into my wallet and handed over a twenty, then hopped out of the car.

She zipped away.

I glanced into P & P, but didn't spot Cass or Del. Connor, wearing one of his usual band T-shirts, finished filling a beer glass and waved. I waved back, then hoofed it down the street to Ancient Magic.

Lights glowed from inside the shop as I neared. All traces of the demons had disappeared from the street, except for a few burn marks from Cass's magic. Even the Magica member's car was gone, thank fates. We didn't like it when they came around the neighborhood.

I pulled open the door and hurried inside. The shop was cluttered and messy, but it was home. Cass and Del were at the shelves, checking on the stock. Cass, with her red hair gleaming in the light, sported her usual brown leather jacket and tall brown boots. Del was dressed entirely in black leather that matched her hair, no doubt having just returned from one of her demon-hunting jobs.

"What's the damage?" I asked.

Del turned, her blue eyes relieved. "Not bad. Just a few broken replicas. The spells that they housed are gone, but none were irreplaceable."

I sagged, grateful.

"Did you get whatever they stole?" Cass asked.

I held up the paper package. "Yep."

"What is it?" Del approached.

I pulled the artifact out of the bag. It was a battered old clay pot. "That bastard. He got an original."

"Weird," Cass said. "No one normally cares if they get the real artifact or a replica."

"What spell has it got?" Del asked.

"I haven't figured that out yet." I inspected the old pot that Cass had brought back from a tomb in northern England just yesterday. It was thousands of years old. From the Beaker culture. "The magic in it is about to blow, which makes it harder to say. Obscures the signature."

All magic decayed with time, eventually becoming so unstable that bad shit happened. Explosions, hordes of locusts, that kinda stuff. Which meant that ancient archaeological sites were basically death traps after a while.

That's where our shop Ancient Magic came in. Cass and Del raided tombs and temples, looking for ancient artifacts that were about to blow and brought them back to the shop. I'd conjure a replica and transfer the magical spell, which we would then sell. The process stabilized the magic, but not indefinitely. The buyer had to use the spell before it went boom, but they usually were quick about it. Once it was all done, the original artifact went back to its archaeological site.

That way, we stayed on the right side of the law and slept easy at night. I'd worked hard on my conjuring. It was my natural, non-FireSoul gift, and no one got weird about Conjurers. They didn't hate them like they hated FireSouls.

And my gift made this whole business possible. It was a good operation. Profitable and entertaining.

Except for the break-ins.

Well, those were entertaining, just not profitable.

Unbidden, the memory of the old man flashed in my mind's eye.

Del's gaze sharpened. "What's wrong?"

"Yeah, you look weird," Cass said.

I sighed. It was impossible to hide anything from these two. Not that I wanted to.

We'd been welded together since we'd woken in a field at fifteen with no memories. We'd struggled to survive—hiding our FireSoul natures while finding our way in a strange world. It'd been hard. Really hard, at times. But we'd made it. Nearly ten years later, we were still stuck at the hip. Though we weren't related by blood, we called each other *deirfiúr*. Sisters in Cass's native Irish. We'd been through everything together—living as runaways, slaves to an evil master, and now as somewhat prosperous businesswomen. We'd come a long way from our shitty beginnings.

"Let's lock this place up, and I'll tell you about it," I said.

When we weren't in the shop, the protective enchantments were so strong that only a nuclear bomb could get in. They were courtesy of Cass's boyfriend, Aidan, who ran a billion-dollar security company. We didn't have the protections running all the time—else how would our customers get in?—but off business hours, this place was on lockdown.

"Let's grab a drink," Cass said. "You look like you could use one."

"Ain't that the truth." I wanted a shower, but I needed to tell them what had happened. I stashed the clay pot behind the desk. I'd transfer the magic tomorrow, and then Cass could return it to the site.

We turned off the lights, and I grabbed my ratty leather jacket before going out onto the street. I shivered as I shrugged into it, only now remembering that it was freaking December in Oregon. The fight and then the murder had kept me occupied, but now, I noticed the cold.

Cass and Del waited as I turned back to the shop and ran my fingertips around the doorjamb. It took about two minutes, but the magic slowly engaged. Unfortunately, it didn't work any faster because it was so strong, but once the spell was ignited, the door was impenetrable.

"Good to go?" Del asked.

I turned to them. "Yep."

As we set off down the street, snow began to fall. Every breath inward made my ribs ache. By the time we reached P & P, I was desperate for a seat and a drink.

Cass pushed the door open, and I followed her into the warmth of our favorite hangout spot. Golden lights housed in mason jars hung from the ceiling, and local art covered the walls. The bar that served coffee in the morning was now kitted out for whiskey and beer.

Connor's music filled the air—something I didn't recognize, but then, I rarely did. It probably was the same band from his T-shirt. He looked up from behind the bar and waved, his lopsided grin familiar. We'd been friends with Connor and his sister, Claire, for the five years we'd lived in Magic's Bend. Connor was a Hearth Witch with a knack for potion making, so he ran P & P most of the time. Since I couldn't see Claire, she had to be off on a mercenary gig for the Order. Her Fire Mage skills made her a good merc, and she was only part-time here at P & P.

Though the bar was cluttered with people, our favorite spot in the corner was still open. The plush chairs never seemed to be occupied, and I was pretty sure someone had enchanted them to repel others. But no one would 'fess up.

Cass glanced at me. "The usual?"

"Yeah." The pain was really getting to me now that the adrenaline had faded. I limped toward the chairs, Del at my side.

"You look like hell, dude," she said.

"Thanks. You're a peach."

"I meant it with love." She smiled.

I pulled her in for a one-arm hug, then immediately regretted it when my ribs sang with pain.

"Sit down, dummy," Del said.

"Yeah, yeah." I sank into the chair, breathing lightly through my lungs.

"Aidan should be here soon," Del said. "He can fix those ribs right up."

"You could tell it was ribs?" I asked.

"Not the first time one of us has cracked ribs."

"True." It was handy that Cass was now dating a guy with a bit of healing power. Much easier than going to the hospital. "How's Roarke?"

"Good," Del said. "In the Underworld, dealing with some business."

Her boyfriend—and it was pretty danged serious between them—was Warden of the Underworld. He kept the peace between the Kings of Hell and made sure that not too many rogue demons made it onto Earth.

Cass returned with the drinks and sank into the chair next to me.

"Here." She handed me the glass. "Drink your medicine."

"Any day." I sipped my Four Roses bourbon on the rocks, while she drank her PBR—the beer of hipsters and hillbillies as she called it. Del sipped her coffee mug of boxed wine. Though we were particular about our beverages, we were cheap. Too many years of being poor while living on the run were hard to break. And now that we actually had a bit of money, it all went into our troves.

"So what's wrong?" Cass asked.

"I witnessed a murder." The memory of the old man appeared in my mind, making my stomach turn.

Del frowned. "Like, a human murder? Not demon?"

The Order of the Magica was fine with us killing demons, since they weren't supposed to be on Earth anyway. But people were another matter.

"A Magica." I explained what had happened with the attacker and the blast of magic.

"What do you think the magic was?" Del asked.

"No idea."

Cass frowned. "Where did it happen?"

"Darklane."

"Hmmm. Bad part of town. You think it's going to be trouble?" Del asked.

"Maybe." Even in Magic's Bend, where weird shit happened all the time, witnessing an outright murder was bad news. "I'm just so pissed that some dude offed an old man. Not cool."

LINSEY HALL

"You're not thinking of hunting down the killer or anything crazy, right?" Cass asked.

I shrugged. I wanted to. I couldn't get the old man's face out of my mind.

"Not a great idea," Del said. "Things have been crazy lately. We should stay under the radar."

Understatement of the century. The last few months had been...active. The three of us were FireSouls—persona non grata in magical society because we could steal powers—so we did our best to lie low. That hadn't been easy lately.

Behind me, the door creaked open, and a cold breeze rushed in. I turned to see Aidan, Cass's boyfriend, walk into the bar. He waved at us, then made his way to the bar, towering over the other customers. He was a good guy, tall and handsome and the strongest Shifter in the world. I couldn't have picked a better match for Cass.

Cass, who was normally tough as steel, was making googly eyes at Aidan's back.

I nudged her with my foot. "Get ahold of yourself."

She grinned. "What? I like him."

"I know." I gestured around the room, grinning. "*Everyone* knows."

She shrugged. "You're just jealous."

"Yeah." I was big enough to admit it. She had a good thing. And as much as I liked my life, I wouldn't say no to a nice dude showing up on my doorstep with dinner and a movie.

Aidan made his way over to us, weaving elegantly through the crowd in the way that only a Shifter could.

"How's it going?" His Scottish accent was strong despite the ten years he'd lived in Magic's Bend. In the time I'd known him, which was only a few months, I'd come to think of him as kind of a brother figure. It was nice. Since I couldn't remember any of my blood family, I'd take what I could get.

Cass jumped up and pressed a quick kiss to his lips. "Great, now that you're here."

"But Nix's ribs could use a blast of your healing power." Del pointed to me.

"Get in a scuffle?" he asked.

"Robbery," I said. "The usual."

Until I'd witnessed a murder.

He raised a brow. "I assume they didn't succeed?"

"Hell no."

Aidan grinned and knelt by my side. "Which ribs?"

I pointed to my left side. He laid a gentle hand on my ribs and fed his warm, healing energy into my side. Besides being a powerful shifter, he had a few Magica gifts as well.

As his gift knitted my bones back together with warm, soothing magic, I was grateful to whatever ancestor had bequeathed him a healing ability.

"Better?" He removed his hand.

"Hundred percent." I shifted and stretched, but there was no pain. "Thanks."

"Anytime." He took a seat next to Cass and picked up his glass of whiskey.

I finished off my drink. "Well, it's been a long day. I think I'm going to take a shower."

Del nodded. "Yeah. Get that blood off you."

I saluted and stood, then made my way out into the cold night. It took only a few minutes to walk down the sidewalk toward our building. We rented the whole factory above our shop, each taking a floor for ourselves.

It was the ideal setup because we all needed a ton of space. FireSouls were said to share the soul of a dragon—though no one really knew what that meant since dragons were long dead. But we did share the dragon's covetousness. Each of us had a treasure trove of our own, made up of whatever weird shit we considered to be valuable. We hoarded it in our apartments, in secret spaces built behind the walls.

Right now, I wanted nothing more than to visit my trove. Not only was it a place to store all my goodies, it was Xanax for the soul. Just sitting amongst my preciouses made me feel a million times calmer, as if the energy reached inside of me like a soothing tonic.

I was basically Gollum—my precious-ing all day long—but hopefully cuter.

I stopped in front of the green door and dug into my pocket for the key. I'd just slid it into the lock when the air changed. Magic crackled, a strange signature that I didn't recognize.

But it was *powerful*. Like, magical nuclear blast powerful. The kind of powerful that could wipe out a city. With me in it.

I could rush inside the building and slam the door behind me, but...nah.

Not my style.

I turned, muscles tensed and ready.

The man who stepped out of the shadows took my breath away. Not just his looks—which were panty-droppingly gorgeous—but the danger that rolled off of him. I could freaking feel it, and that was unusual.

It felt like hungry tigers were circling me.

He kept to the shadows near a broken lamp post—in fact, he almost looked like he was made of shadow.

That had to be his magic. Supernatural's power gave off different signatures that lit up the senses. Strong supernaturals triggered more than one sense. This guy triggered all five.

And the first one I noticed was that he looked like he could blend in with any of his surroundings. His form almost looked transparent—but he was still so real. A human chameleon.

He was tall and broad shouldered, the kind of guy who looked like he chopped down trees for a living or built great iron bridges. But his face was far too sophisticated for either of those options. He looked like a damned fallen angel, and I was dead certain those didn't exist.

But the magic that rolled off him was almost dark. It smelled like a cold winter morning and felt like a hot caress against my skin. It was the flickering of flames, but wonderful. It even banished the chill in the air.

"You're the one I seek." His voice rolled over me like waves, deep and strong. His accent was a little bit like Russian, but not quite.

And he wanted me? Yikes. I held up a hand. "Hang on."

He raised a dark brow and looked at me, curiosity gleaming in his eyes, as if I were something unexpected. Not used to being talked back to?

Good. I liked being unexpected. And I had to get a feel for the rest of his magical signature. I needed to know what he was.

Dangerous, that was for sure. But what *was* he?

As subtly as I could, I called my magic up from within. I was careful to repress my own signature for fear that he would sense what I was doing. Powerful supernaturals could control how much of a signature they gave off. He was definitely strong enough to do that, though he clearly didn't want to.

This guy wanted me to know how strong he was.

Don't worry, pal. I get it.

His magic tasted like the best whiskey, rich and warm with a slight burn. Seductive. And the sound was that of a thunderstorm rolling in the distance.

"You about done?" His voice was as deep and sexy as before. And scary.

I shivered.

With his dark jeans and sleek brown leather jacket, he'd look just like a regular guy if regular guys looked like killer super models.

He led with his power, the magical equivalent of swinging his dick around.

"You mean business, don't you?" I asked.

"Always."

"What the hell are you?"

His green eyes darkened. "A problem for you."

Yeah, that was the truth. I kept my magic primed, just below the surface of my skin. It prickled and jumped, ready to be set free. But I wouldn't, not until I knew I'd have to fight. Because once you conjured a weapon, people knew what was coming.

And I didn't want to give this guy a head start. My magic was weaker from all the conjuring I'd done all day. I'd need to rest to completely rejuvenate.

"I mean what species? I don't like games," I said.

"Are you sure?" His voice was so deeply seductive that I'd have to be dead not to get his drift. And from the way my insides lit up, I was certainly not dead. Every part of me was brilliantly alive —with the desire to fuck and flee, I couldn't figure out which.

And *all* of that was a bad idea. This guy was a predator. You didn't flee from predators, and you certainly didn't fuck them.

I was impulsive, not stupid.

"I don't want to play *your* games," I corrected.

He grinned, his full lips curving up in a smile that devastated my insides. It was a nuclear bomb that laid waste to my good sense.

Until he stepped forward. Those few feet gave me a chance to really get a feel for his magic. The chill scent of a winter morning, the hot caress of a hand brushing my arm.

And something else. Something I'd only ever heard about but not felt. A prick against my neck—lovely and terrible at the same time.

My stomach dropped out of me. "You're a vampire."

"*The* vampire." He stepped closer, now only a dozen feet away.

The earth tilted even more on its axis as I picked up a sixth signature. My dragon sense pulled me toward him.

What the hell?

My dragon sense was a gift from my FireSoul side. It allowed me to find things of value. Treasure. Dragons loved treasure.

But it'd never pulled me toward a *person* before.

And it chose this moment to pull me toward *him*?

It was clearly mistaken.

"What do you mean, *the* vampire?" My heart raced as I searched his features, trying to get a glimpse of his fangs. But they stayed hidden behind his too-perfect lips.

"This."

The air around him shimmered, as if he were dropping some kind of concealment charm.

I staggered back against the door, hit by more magic than I'd ever sensed on a single being before. His every magical signature was multiplied by a hundred. I'd already thought he was strong. But this was nuts.

"Shit," I breathed. "No wonder you keep that under wraps."

He wasn't just a vampire. There was more magic to him. But what?

"So you know who I am?" Quiet confidence gleamed in his brilliant green eyes.

"Yeah." I swallowed hard, suddenly cursing my decision to leave the bar early. "You're the Enforcer. The most powerful vampire alive."

I didn't know much about vampires, but I'd heard of him. Goosebumps prickled my skin, and fear curdled in my belly. Most supernaturals were governed by either the Alpha Council—for the shifters—or the Order of the Magica—for the rest of us. But vampires had their own governing body.

In all my life, I'd only ever seen one other vampire. They were highly secretive and rarely interacted with other supernaturals. That guy had been nothing like this one. This one... He was *unique.*

As beautiful as he was, he was even more dangerous. I'd only ever heard whispered rumors of the Enforcer who both protected vampires and policed them in equal measures. He was death on the wind, so fast and strong that you didn't see him coming.

The fact that he was here, talking to me….

That was enough to scare the sense out of anyone.

"Why are you at my door?" I asked. "It's been a long day, and I'm ready for bed."

I almost thought interest sparked in his eyes, but they quickly turned cold. "Does murder exhaust you?"

CHAPTER THREE

I barked a laugh, but fear rose in my belly, a toxic mess that made me want to hurl. "I have no idea what you're talking about."

"Of course you do. You murdered Marin Olerafort. Your magic was all over the scene. All over the weapon."

Shit. I'd done a piss-poor job covering my tracks, apparently. But who'd have thought a supernatural bloodhound would be on the case? I wanted to conjure a weapon, but my odds of winning a fight against this guy were ridiculously slim.

"I didn't murder him." Sweat rolled down my spine. "I tried to save him."

"You did a poor job of that."

"I know."

"Your magic was on the blade. You sunk it into his heart."

"I didn't!" But shit, this looked bad. I never should have used my conjuring at the scene. I'd left my signature all over the place. "I conjured a towel to try to stop the flow of blood."

"Then where is it?"

"In a dumpster near the alley."

"That's convenient. The leading theory amongst the Vampire

Court is that you conjured the blade and that's why your magic was on it."

"I didn't! And I saw the murderer."

Skepticism flashed on his face. "What did he look like?"

"I don't know. It was far away. Bigger than Marin, and wearing a cloak."

"A cloaked figure?" He laughed derisively. "That gives me nothing. And it doesn't help you."

No, it didn't. I could give him nothing more than the obvious, and that wasn't believable. Not with my magic at the scene.

"What were you doing in the Shadowlands?" he asked. "You shouldn't even be able to enter that realm."

"What the hell are the Shadowlands?" Was he talking about the darkness that had pervaded the alley?

His brows lowered over his eyes. "You're a strange one." He stepped closer, until he was only a half dozen feet away. His eyes gleamed with interest as they traced over my face. "What are you?"

I shrugged. "Conjurer. Nothing exciting."

"Oh, that's hardly true."

I scowled. "Fine. I may be exciting, but I'm just a Conjurer."

"That's only half true."

I swallowed hard. "The exciting part?"

"That part is true. The *only a Conjurer* part is bollocks. You're something different. I can sense it."

Shit. I didn't want him sensing what I really was. There was a bounty on FireSoul heads. Though the Enforcer was rumored to be super rich—even he might like the cash that the Order of the Magica would give him for turning me in. Or the social connections. The governments didn't always cooperate. But if he brought me to them? He'd be favored, no question.

"Dude, I have no idea what you are talking about." I stepped back until I was pressed against the door. "I didn't kill your friend. I know nothing about the person who did. And I'm ready to go to bed."

This time, interest definitely sparked in his eyes. And it took longer to fade. In fact, he seemed like he had to force it away until anger simmered in his eyes.

He was pissed about this Marin guy's murder. But he was also interested in me. In getting me into bed?

Nah. Though he was so damned hot that if he was a normal guy, I'd have considered it. Except that he was terrifying. Terrifying was *so* not my thing. And he was the farthest thing from normal.

Just like my life was going to be if he insisted that I'd killed Marin.

"I'm here to take you before the Vampire Court. You've hereby been accused of the murder of Marin Olerafort."

"I didn't do it!" *Shit!* This was getting too real.

"Then why can I sense fear on you? The innocent wouldn't be fearful."

A derisive laugh escaped me. "You're joking, right? You just said you'd drag me in front of the Vampire Court. Anyone who isn't an idiot would get a little nervous."

Not to mention, I'd have my own government after me if they knew I was a FireSoul. And that would put Cass and Del at risk, as well. Why did he even care? Marin hadn't been a vampire.

All of this was going south.

"Here's an idea," I said. "My friend Connor is the best potions maker around. He works right down the street. Let's go there. He can whip up a truth serum in no time. I'll take it, then I'll tell you everything I know. And you'll see I'm telling the truth."

Skepticism lowered his brow. "I'm not going to trust your friend."

"You can watch him make it. You can even consult the recipe book. He'll use a standard one, approved by the Order of the Magica."

"Even those aren't infallible. Everyone knows that. Truth serums are best used when the victim doesn't see it coming. Otherwise, they can erect mental defenses."

Damn it. This guy was stubborn. He was also right.

Which meant I had no freaking clue how to get him to believe me. Add in his suspicion of my species and the fact that I could "walk in the Shadowlands"—whatever that meant—it wasn't looking good for me.

And I did *not* want to go in front of the Vampire Court. They were a shadowy organization that I knew nearly nothing about. But vampires were rumored to have a mind reader on their court. I didn't need them reading my mind and figuring out that I was more than just a nobody Conjurer.

A cell phone vibrated, the sound coming from the Enforcer's pocket. His expression hardly changed, but I'd have swore I saw a hint of a frown.

He reached into his pocket and pulled out a big cuff made of gold.

A millisecond later, he appeared in front of me and snapped the golden cuff around my neck. Magic fizzed through it. My heart thundered and my skin chilled.

I punched him, but hit only air.

His head had dodged left, too quickly for me to see. He reached out and pinned me to the door, his hand hard against my chest. I kicked and thrashed, but his vampire speed was too great for me. He avoided every strike.

Rage welled within me, a fiery burn.

It only increased when he pulled his still vibrating phone from his pocket and put it to his ear. All while holding me to the door with one long arm.

"Bastard!" I called on my magic, conjuring a sword and thrusting it toward his belly.

Quick as a snake, he dodged. I sliced the blade again, but he let go of me and knocked my sword arm so hard that it went numb. I dropped the blade.

He grasped both my wrists and pinned my arms above my head, pressing the full length of his hard body against mine to keep me from kicking him.

Then he put the phone back to his ear.

"You son of a fucking Horrabeast! Let me go!"

He ignored me, listening to the person on the other end of the line. His body was hot and hard against mine, all strength and tension keeping me trapped against the wall. He was so close that I could feel his heartbeat against my chest. Vampires weren't dead like human fiction said they were, though they did drink blood to survive.

He towered over me, so tall that my head didn't top his shoulder. I considered biting him, but my teeth wouldn't make it through his leather jacket.

And I really didn't want to go for his neck, even if I could reach it. That wouldn't turn me into a vampire, but I didn't want to put any neck-biting ideas into his head. Not with my own neck so close to his fangs.

Though I strained my ears, I couldn't hear anything that the other person on the line said. I thrashed, trying to get away, but it did no good.

"Are you sure?" the Enforcer said.

Damn it, what the hell was his name? Like all super scary badasses, he went by a title in public. Cass was dating the Origin. Del dated the Warden.

I *seriously* doubted I'd be dating the Enforcer. Trying to kill him, sure. Dating, no way.

I could not believe my dragon sense had pulled toward this guy. It'd gone haywire.

Finally, he hung up.

"Done?" I gave my tone as much acid as I could muster.

"Hardly." His green eyes were cold when they met mine.

I shifted, desperate to get away from this stone-cold killer. The movement rubbed a few of my more interesting bits against his.

And he noticed.

His gaze darkened. Warmed a bit. I swallowed hard. The tension in the air turned thick as pudding.

I dragged in a heavy breath. "What the hell is this thing around my neck?"

"Insurance. You're the official suspect in a murder investigation. The Vampire Court is quick in issuing its verdicts. In three days, if you haven't been cleared, that thing will blow your head off."

"What!" I shrieked the words, thrashing and kicking like a banshee. "You son of a bitch!"

"We can't have you running off," he said. "Particularly now that I have to go check on something."

"What the hell? Ever heard of innocent until proven guilty?"

"Not in the vampire court. And that thing will keep you from making a run for it while I figure this out. Cheaper than jail cells."

"What do you have to check on? You're just going to leave me here wearing this murder collar?"

He nodded, his gaze deadly serious. "Yeah. It's procedure. You're the number one suspect and this keeps you at hand. Added to that, you can walk in the Shadowlands. That is forbidden to your kind. I want to know why you can trespass like that."

"I didn't trespass!"

"You did. Was it because of your strange magic?"

"I have no idea what you're talking about."

"Of course you do." His gaze turned hard. "Fortunately, with that collar on you, running is out of the question. I'll have time to figure out your secrets."

I swallowed hard, shivers racing over my skin. This was so not good. Because he was right. I did have secrets. Dangerous one. And I didn't want him to figure them out.

"I'll be back soon," he said. "There will be guards on your place. An extra incentive to not leave. In case you decide to get stupid."

"Guards?"

He waved a hand, a subtle gesture. Two vampires melted out of the shadows in the distance. I had to peer around his shoulder to see them fully. They'd been hiding near the park, in the shadows of the bushes, and I'd been so freaked out by the Enforcer that I hadn't noticed them.

Bad Nix.

That kind of laziness could get me killed.

Especially with a murder collar around my neck.

Boy, had I played this one poorly. Demons were no problem. Enforcer vampires? Apparently they were a problem for me.

The two vampires stopped on the other side of the street, their gazes on me. They weren't as big as the Enforcer and their magic didn't feel as strong, but I still didn't want to tangle with them.

Vampire guards, murder collar. Sweat dripped down my spine despite the cold night.

"They'll stay there until I return. Don't leave your apartment. If you could even manage to get by them"—he gave my vampire Hello Kitty T-shirt a curious glance, as if he couldn't figure me out—"it will take nothing for me to track you down. And don't forget about the collar. You must appear in front of the Vampire Court within three days or...boom."

I swallowed hard, believing every word. That was his job. Hunting people. Both vampires who did wrong and those who hurt any vampires under his dominion.

"How do I find the Vampire Court?"

"You don't. I take you."

"Fine." I bit out the word, equal parts annoyed and freaked out. Hopefully my friends could get me out of this. "But other people live here as well. They have to be able to come home."

"They can enter. But the guards won't let you leave."

My jaw hardened. We'd see about that.

"Okay." Forcing out the words was like prying open a new jar.

He gave me one last look, then stepped back and disappeared into thin air. Immediately, I was cold, my muscles like jelly. I leaned heavily against the door, panting and eyeing the vampires.

Shit, shit, shit.

When I'd said I wanted a hot guy to show up on my doorstep, this hadn't been what I'd meant. He thought I'd killed that guy Marin. And he'd sensed strange magic on me. No one was able to do that. I kept my true self hidden deep.

But he'd sensed it. And he wanted to drag me in front of the Vampire Court. He *would* drag me in front of the Vampire Court, or this collar would blow my head off.

I reached up, tugging at it. The thing didn't budge. It was smooth and warm beneath my fingertips. Normally, gold gave me the warm fuzzies. It gave all FireSouls the warm fuzzies.

Not this thing.

Shaking, I turned and unlocked the green door, then made my way up the long flight of stairs to my apartment, which was right above the shop. Del lived above me, and Cass above her.

I let myself into my cluttered home. This part was nothing special, just one thousand square feet of Goodwill furniture and an old kitchen with a fridge that liked to sing me the song of its people. The hums and whines kept me company.

But even the eighteen-pound block of English cheddar that I kept in that fridge wouldn't fix me in an emergency like this. Every muscle I had felt like a noodle, and my mind was racing like it wanted to win the Indie 500.

Cass, Del, and I had come close to discovery in the past. They'd had a few particularly close run-ins. But I was *excellent* at hiding my magical signature and lying low—I'd never come so close personally.

With the Enforcer on my tail, I was well into the deep end here.

I pressed my fingertips to the comms charm at my neck. "Cass? Del? I have a problem."

Del answered immediately. "Where are you?"

"My apartment."

"We'll be right there," Cass said.

"Ignore the vampires across the street and let yourself in. I'll be in my trove." I cut off the connection and hurried to my bedroom. It was small and cave-like, with one window leading out onto an alley. The mirror above the dresser showed the narrow gold collar around my neck.

I ignored it and went to the empty wall, where I pressed my fingertips to the plaster and envisioned the wall disappearing. It ignited the magic, and a doorway appeared. I left it open for Cass and Del and stepped inside.

There was just a spiral staircase leading upward. The rest of the space was empty and dark. Though Cass and Del stored their troves in the big empty spaces behind their bedroom walls, that wouldn't work for mine. The only thing back here was the stairway.

I began to climb, three stories up to the roof, where I stepped out into the jungle. Plants of every variety grew in profusion. We'd built this space custom when we'd moved in, creating a giant greenhouse that was enchanted to be hidden from view. From the outside, it looked like a normal roof.

It was far from normal.

This was where I really lived. Though I slept and ate and watched TV out in the main part of the apartment, this cavernous three-thousand square foot space was my heart. My home.

My trove.

I gazed out over the giant room that contained my treasures.

I'd been collecting since we'd moved in here five years ago. It was the first time I'd had a place to store my preciouses.

It was a weird place, considering that it was a jungle and there were three cars in the space. They'd had to be magically transported inside and the building strengthened with enchantments.

Treasure was different for each of us. For me, it was plants, cars, and weapons of every variety. I kept the weapons because my conjuring required that I fully understand the thing I was creating. By getting to know so many different weapons, I was able to conjure anything and protect myself. It was really more of a survival mechanism, but I loved the gleaming blades and elegant bows. They were stored on shelves in the back of the greenhouse.

I had the cars just because I liked them. Up here, I had a '71 Plymouth RoadRunner, a '68 Pontiac FireBird, and a '69 Ford Mustang Boss 429. They sat in the middle of the greenhouse, paint gleaming.

Since it was hard for me to get them out of here—I had to buy an expensive transportation spell—they mostly just sat here. But I loved them.

The plants—they were my babies. I'd always loved growing things, but I'd never had the ability until we'd moved to Factory Row and created this space. The glass ceiling let in light, but I also had grow lights for the plants that wanted more sun.

Trees and bushes and flowers bloomed in profusion, filling the place with the most amazing scent. I didn't know why I loved plants so much, but a while ago I'd heard a prophecy about how I was somehow connected to the magic of life.

It made no sense to me, so I ignored it. There were more important things to focus on, anyway.

I walked among the plants, checking the irrigation tubing and pinching off some dead buds. My breathing calmed just being in here. I was a great big dragon-y stereotype, but I didn't care.

This place wouldn't protect me for long, though. Not with this thing around my neck.

I heard footsteps on the stairs and turned to see Cass and Del entering climbing up from the stairs. Aidan wasn't with them, probably because he knew he wasn't allowed in my trove. Too personal. Though I thought of him as a brother, it still would have been weird.

"What the hell is up with the vampires across the street?" Del asked.

"Does this have to do with the murder?" Cass frowned.

"Yeah." I pointed to my neck.

Their gazes went immediately to the collar. In unison, they asked, "What is that?"

I explained what had just happened.

"Shit. The Enforcer?" Del asked. "Here? After you?"

Cass had gone entirely white, her red hair now stark against her skin. "That collar is bad fucking news."

"No kidding." I paced the open space in front of the shelves, my hands wrapped around my arms. "Do you think there is any way to take it off?"

"I don't know." Cass dug her phone out of her pocket. "Let's ask people smarter than us."

"Good idea." I held still—as still as I could, while shaking—and let Cass take a close up picture of the collar.

"I'm sending this to Dr. Garriso," she said. "And Aidan and Roarke, for good measure."

"Good." I touched it again, unable to help myself. One of those three might know what was up. Both Aidan and Roarke had contacts with the magical governments, so they might know something about vampires.

And Dr. Garriso was our friend at the Museum for Magical History in downtown Magic's Bend. The old scholar knew something about everything.

"Send it to Aerdeca and Mordaca, too," Del said.

Cass nodded.

"Good idea," I said. Aerdeca and Mordaca were sister blood sorceresses who lived in Darklane. They often knew all kinds of weird things.

"While we wait for responses, tell us where the Enforcer went," Cass said.

"No idea. But when he comes back, he's going to drag me in front of the Vampire Court. This collar will make sure I show up."

"Oh shit," Del said. "They might be able to sense what you are. Vampires are weird like that. They've got a mind reader, right? And they're good at feeling out magic."

"It'd be almost impossible to stop it," Cass said. "The Vampire Court is too powerful. And we have no sway there. None."

Cass's boyfriend had an in with the Alpha Council, and Del's had an in with the Order of the Magica. But no one knew anyone within the Vampire Court. No one *wanted* to know anyone within the Vampire Court.

"Fuck." I rubbed my hand over my eyes. "I need to prove I'm innocent."

"That needs to happen before you even go in front of the Court," Del said.

"Seconded." Cass's phone vibrated, and she pulled it out and studied it. "Neither Roarke nor Aidan know how to remove the collar."

My heart sank. The phone vibrated twice, and I looked at her hopefully.

She studied her phone, then looked up at me. "Both Aerdeca and Mordaca and Dr. Garriso say that there is no way to remove the collar short of being a member of the Vampire Court."

My shoulders sagged. "Shit."

"Shit is right," Del said. "So we need to find some clues."

"Yeah." I straightened and nodded. Moping wasn't going to

get me anywhere. "I need to find at least one clue to point him in another direction. That might buy me some time."

It was the only option that made sense. And I still wanted to find Marin's killer. The image of his face hadn't left me. I wanted justice as well as my own freedom. Leaving him there had felt like shit.

"How do you solve a murder, though?" Del asked.

"I've got this," I said. "I've seen plenty of police shows. And *The Fugitive*. Hell, I'm basically Harrison Ford here."

Cass frowned. "Better to be Harrison in his role as Indy, though."

"No kidding." With our treasure-hunting gig, we normally were Indiana Joneses. I wanted to get back to that—not be on the run for my life. "This will be fine. I know what to do."

At least, I freaking hoped I did.

CHAPTER FOUR

My plan started with an escape attempt, as many good plans often do. A quick peek out my bedroom window confirmed that there were vampire guards surrounding my place.

The Enforcer was taking no chances. He clearly hadn't fallen for my Hello Kitty T-shirt.

Which meant he took me seriously, and that was a major pain in the ass right now. I'd have preferred to sneak down the alley because he hadn't properly secured the perimeter. Instead, I was waiting for Connor to show up with a couple of sleeping potions. He could whip up anything—acid bombs, fire blasts, stunning drafts. Even quick-acting sleeping potions.

I used the waiting time to sneak in a quick shower and upgrade to my 'Lil Bub T-shirt. I loved that weird little internet cat. I was tying my shoes when I heard footsteps thunder from the stairs leading up to my place.

I went into the living room, where Cass and Del were opening the door to Connor. He lifted the bag, a big grin on his face. Today, his band T-shirt was for Lyle Lovett. I approved.

"Got 'em! Two sleeping bombs and an invisibility potion for good measure." His British accent was thick despite the five years he'd lived in Magic's Bend. "Can't stay long though. Claire is minding the bar, and you know how she is."

"More focused on demon killing than drink slinging," I said.

"Exactly." He shook his head. "Can't trust her around the taps."

"Thanks for bringing those." I dug money out of the little wallet that I'd shoved into my jeans and traded him for the bag of potion bombs. "You're a lifesaver."

"Happy to help!"

"The sleeping potions will only last a few hours, right?"

"Yeah. They're for the vampires out front?"

"Exactly. I don't want them sleeping when the sun comes up and turning into crispy critters." Though vampires scared the crap out of me—all that biting and blood—they weren't free game like demons. The last thing I needed was an actual murder charge.

"Don't you worry." Connor winked. "They'll wake in time."

"Thanks," I said. "Want to wait until they are asleep to pass back by them?"

He grinned. "Nah, they don't bother me. I'll go now. Save my precious taps from my sister's wayward mind."

"You're one tough duck, Connor." He was only twenty-two and a Hearth Witch, but Hearth Witches were tough, no matter what anyone said.

"I'll be going. Good luck with the vampires."

"Thanks. I'm gonna need it."

He turned and left, pounding down the stairs and out into the cold night.

I dug into the bag and pulled out a sleeping bomb. The potion was contained in a blue glass ball that would explode on impact, drenching the unwitting vampire in a sleeping potion that should knock him out.

I handed it to Cass. "You're the best at throwing things."

"I won't be offended," Del said.

"Good. Because you're a badass with that sword."

Cass went to the window and peered out. I joined her, pulling my own potion bomb out of the bag. I tucked the vial of invisibility potion into my pocket. I wouldn't use it unless absolutely necessary. They tasted like crap and were hard to come by.

Cass pointed to the two vampires loitering below. "We can hit them, no problem."

"Yeah, they're probably only forty feet away." Even better, their gazes were glued on the first floor door, not up higher where we were.

"Excellent." Del rubbed her hands together. "Let's get this show started, then we can sneak out and solve a murder."

I grinned at her, then turned back to the window.

"Del, could you use your gift to suppress sound?" I asked. "I don't want the vampires to hear us open the windows."

"Sure thing." Del approached the windows. She'd stolen the power from a creepy demon a couple months ago. Just the thought made me shudder, though she suffered no ill effects.

Cass and I each took up position at one of the two big windows. Del's magic flared briefly on the air, bringing with it the scent of fresh soap. She nodded to us.

I bit my lip as I eased the window up. There wasn't the usual creak of old wood and metal, so I relaxed. Once the windows were all the way open, cold winter air rushed into the apartment.

I glanced at Cass, who nodded at me and mouthed, *on three.*

I nodded back, and we counted. At three, I hurled my potion bomb at the vampire closest to me. He never saw it coming.

The glass ball exploded on his chest, splashing him with a pale blue liquid. Cass's potion bomb found its mark, and her demon swayed along with mine. They both crashed to the pavement, a weird synchronized ballet.

"Nice one." I shut the window and hurried to the door. "Now let's get this party started."

I grabbed a clean jacket and my car keys from the hook by the door and hurried down the stairs. Del and Cass were right behind me.

The air was bitter cold and the night dark when I exited the building. My gaze went immediately to the vampires, who were dead asleep on the sidewalk, looking like drunks who'd wandered away from the bar.

"This way." I turned left. "Fabio is over here."

We headed toward the car I drove around town, which was parked on the other side of the road a few yards down. Fabio was a Dodge Challenger Hellcat, a ridiculously powerful muscle car that spoke to my soul.

We piled in, Del in the front with me and Cass in the back.

Since it was late and we wanted to be sneaky, I pressed the Stealth Mode button that would magically dampen the sound of the roaring engine. Fabio had quite the growl, but it wasn't always appropriate. Certainly not when one was trying to creep away from sleeping vampires. Fabio started as silently as a Tesla, and I took off away from the curb.

"Where in Darklane are we going?" Cass asked.

"Fair Fortune Alley."

"Seriously?" Cass asked. "Fair Fortune Alley is where you had your worst streak of luck to date?"

"Yep." I sighed. "Let's just hope my luck turns around."

I sped through the quiet streets of Magic's Bend. It was after nine, so folks were either home or plunked down on their favorite barstools. The dead-empty business district and bustling bars of the historic district just proved my point.

"We really ought to come down here more often," Del said as we cruised past a particularly hopping place called The Drunken Troll.

"Let's get Nix off the hook first." I turned toward Darklane.

It was quieter here, with only a few shadowy individuals skulking along the sidewalk. The buildings were as old as those in the historic district, but instead of the brightly colored paint that made that part of town so charming, the buildings in Darklane were covered with a thick layer of dark soot. It could just be dirt, but my money was on the residue of dark magic.

I pulled the car over into an empty spot near the curb, right behind a hearse. I wasn't going to read into that.

We climbed out. The chill hit me hard, and I zipped my jacket to ward off the bite. We were on the main street in Darklane, but most of the lights in the buildings were dimmed. Only half of the streetlamps worked.

It was creepy and kooky and all together spooky—entirely suited for the Addams family. And though the residents here were often on the wrong side of the law and we tried to avoid that kind of thing, some of our closest friends lived and worked here.

"This way." I hunched my shoulders against the wind and led the way down the street toward Fair Fortune Alley. "Once we're in the alley, we can use our dragon senses to look for clues."

"Should we split up?" Del asked.

"Probably." I dodged a puddle of green slime. "Don't want to draw attention. And if we have to knock on any doors, best not to do it as a group. The residents here probably don't like to be startled after dusk."

"Good plan," Cass said.

Though we didn't look like much more than your average twenty-something women and this place screamed *danger!*, we were the things that went bump in the night here. No matter how many murderous demons or wicked warlocks prowled the streets of Darklane, we could hold our own.

Except against vampire Enforcers. But I wouldn't think of my poor showing right now.

I turned down Fair Fortune Alley and glanced back at Del and Cass. "See you guys in an hour?"

"Yep." Del nodded. "Use your comms charm if you need us."

I saluted, then turned back to the alley and stepped inside.

Suddenly, the world went darker and quieter than it had been a moment ago. I took a few steps, trying to shake it off. But the narrow, cobblestoned alley still had a creepy feel to it. Like it had earlier this evening.

I turned back to ask Del and Cass to see if they felt the same thing, but they were gone. That was fast. Their dragon senses must have already picked up on something.

I shrugged and crept farther down the alley. The ground that had been torn apart by the demon was roughly mended, though still clearly in need of some attention.

Who had repaired it so quickly? Magic's Bend municipal services weren't exactly quick, and this was Darklane. They'd let this place fall into the nearby sea before they did much to repair this part of town.

I stored the question for later and called upon my dragon sense. It was the only FireSoul gift I used, and even then, I used it rarely. Just to help find items for my trove, normally.

Ideally, you'd have information about what you sought. What it looked like, smelled like, tasted like, its origin. Anything. But if you were desperate, you could jumpstart it with your desire alone. In those cases, it didn't give you the exact answer—but it might point you in the right direction or give some clues.

Since I was really freaking desperate, the magic within me ignited, then warmed and curled, like a fog that filled my limbs and mind.

Who killed Marin Olerafort?

I wished I'd gotten a good look at him to help my dragon sense, but I had nothing more than an image of a large cloaked figure.

So I repeated the question, along with the scene of his death, until my dragon sense latched on to something. It pulled at my middle, directing me farther down the alley. Toward where Marin's body had once been.

He was no longer there, nor was any evidence of his death.

It'd been about three hours, and apparently whoever had cared for him was quick.

I passed the dumpster where I'd killed the demon, but his body was long gone too.

My dragon sense pulled me toward the side street where Marin and his attacker had come from. It was an even narrower street, but it showed the fronts of buildings rather than the backs like in Fair Fortune Alley. The moon hung low over the sky at the end of the road, shedding its watery light over the ramshackle buildings.

I hurried down the street, conscious that the Enforcer could come looking for me at any moment. Given what little information I had about the killer, it was unlikely my dragon sense would lead me straight to him. But if I could get even a clue...

I needed just one—anything—to put the Enforcer off my trail.

Plump rats skittered along the side of the road, pressing themselves close to the edge of the building. They squeaked as they passed me. A warning or a greeting?

On my left, a narrow black door called to me. The building above was one of the newer ones on the street. It was brick and flat-fronted—probably only two hundred years old.

I eyed it warily. The windows looked almost blank, like no one lived within. But if this was where my dragon sense pulled me...

Warily, I knocked.

The wind whistled down the street as I waited, the silent moon my only company. I almost wished the rats would come back.

An electric charge filled the air, the subtle tang of magic being ignited. I braced myself, letting my magic wait at the ready. I didn't have a lot left—I *really* needed a nap after today—but I could get myself out of whatever was coming at me.

"Who's there?" a reedy voice demanded.

I glanced around. The door hadn't opened, so who the hell was that?

"Hello?" I said.

"Who are you?" There was still no figure to match the voice. That had to be the magic that I'd felt. Someone was projecting their voice, like a magical intercom.

Probably an older woman, from the sound of it.

"I'm Phoenix Knight."

"Fancy name."

"Yeah." I'd chosen it myself when I'd woken in the field at fifteen with Cass and Del. We'd looked to the sky and chosen our names from the constellations. Cass was Cassiopeia, Del was Delphinus, and I'd chosen Phoenix, hoping to rise from the ashes of whatever my terrible past had done to me. I didn't remember that past, but the stomach-churning sickness I'd gotten whenever I'd tried to remember had made me certain it was shit.

"I'm here to ask some questions," I said.

"That'll cost you."

"What do you want?" *Please let it be something I could conjure.* I was nearly broke from the last ancient map I'd bought for my collection. Though our shop did well, Cass, Del and I were almost constantly broke because we were feeding our treasure-hunting beasts.

"Chuckles."

"Chuckles? Like, the candy?"

"Yes. They've been discontinued. There's no way to get Chuckles any longer, and I find that I fancy them." She cackled.

Was the old bat screwing with me?

If so, she'd picked the wrong discontinued candy. I happened to like Chuckles. A lot. The gooey, chemical fruitiness was one of my favorite treats.

And because I was well-familiar with them, I'd hit the jackpot.

"No problem," I said. "I can bring you Chuckles. Right now, in fact."

"Now?" Suspicion laced her voice.

"Yep. Just let me in, answer my questions, and I'll give them to you."

"Let me see."

See? I glanced up at the windows to see if she was peering down, but they were just as dead-empty as they had been.

"Do it!" she demanded.

"All right!" I called on my magic, conjuring a crinkly plastic package of the discontinued candy. I held it up. "See!"

"They'd better taste right." The mistrust in her voice made me grin.

"They will. I'm a pro. And there's more where that came from if you can answer my questions."

"Follow the cat, then."

"The cat?" What the hell?

"And you'd better have pure intentions."

Pure intentions?

The door in front of me creaked open, and a stocky black tomcat peered out. He had a bruiser's face and medium-length fur that stuck out at all angles. His mouth opened to reveal bright white fangs and a deep meow, then he turned abruptly.

"Okay, then." I followed him inside.

But it wasn't actually *inside* anything at all. The door led to a hollowed-out old building with crazy black plants growing wild within. Along the wall, a rickety iron staircase led up. It wrapped around the inside of the building, leading up to nowhere, as far as I could see.

"Did a bomb go off in here?" I asked the cat.

"Meerow."

"Yes?"

"Meerow."

Since that answer sounded no different than the other, it was hard to say. All I could do was follow the cat, so I did. He led me toward the stairs and started upward.

At the base of the stairs, the black plants curled around the spindles of the iron stair railing. My fingertips itched to pet their silky black leaves. I reached out, desire curling deep in my belly.

I just wanted to brush my hand against them. Just once.

My dragon sense tugged hard, away from the leaves.

I shook it off, annoyed, and reached out for the leaves.

But it tugged harder, finally breaking through the weird haze in my mind. I glanced at the cat. He'd stopped climbing the stairs and was watching me intently, curiosity in his green eyes.

"Something's wrong with these leaves, isn't there?" I asked.

This time, he didn't meow, leaving me to make up my own mind. Though I still wanted to touch the leaves, I curled my hands into fists and kept them tucked at my sides.

She'd booby-trapped the entrance to her home. After the weird magical voice trick, I shouldn't be surprised.

"Lead on," I said to the cat.

"Meerow." He turned and trotted up the stairs.

We climbed two stories, winding our way around the interior of the hollowed-out building. There was at least another story to go when the stairs in front of me split into two separate staircases. And there were two separate cats.

Both turned to stare at me.

Shit. "Which one of you is the real cat?"

They blinked, looking identical. Dang it. Another test. Or trap.

I licked my lips and concentrated. It was never smart to pick the wrong one.

What had the old woman said? Make sure your intentions are pure?

"I just want to ask questions." I held up the candy. "And I have Chuckles."

The cats just stared at me. So I conjured two more packs of Chuckles and thought really hard about just asking questions and leaving not so much as a dusty footprint on her front doormat.

53

Eventually, the stairs in front of me shimmered. One disappeared, along with its cat, which had clearly been an illusion.

In their place was nothing but a thirty-foot drop and more broken ribs.

I heaved out a sigh. "So I passed?"

"Meerow."

"That sounds more like 'don't screw this up' than 'well done.'"

"Meerow."

Yep, that was cat for 'don't screw this up.'

He turned and led the way farther up. I followed. The stairs terminated at a door. One single eye was painted on the surface, with eyelashes made of knives. Yikes.

But the windows on either side of the door had window boxes full of geraniums. Quite the contrast.

I kinda liked this lady already.

I raised my hand to knock, but the door swung open before I could. Tom raced in, joining two other cats on a red rug in the middle of the floor. All were identical.

A woman stepped out from behind the door. There was something odd about her. An air that I couldn't quite place.

"Chuckles?" Her voice was creaky and old, but she didn't look a day over sixty. And a well-put-together sixty at that. She had wild auburn hair streaked with white and was dressed like a fortune-teller from a movie. Full skirts of many colors and golden chains.

The house behind her was brightly decorated as well, with plush fabrics and velvets that made it look like a sultan's pleasure den in the Middle East.

"Hi." I held out one of the packages of Chuckles.

She took it with a hand tipped with red talons, then laughed, low in her throat.

"Oh my god, did you just chuckle?" I asked.

Her dark brows dropped low over her green eyes. "That was a terrible pun."

I shrugged. "I'm the worst. So sue me."

"Wouldn't bother. You're broke." Her gaze snapped to the collar around my neck. "And in trouble, from the looks of it."

"Yeah."

"You're the walking dead."

"Uh, no."

"That collar says otherwise. Vampire quarry."

I swallowed hard. "That's why I have questions. Can I come in?"

She stepped back. "I'll be expecting more Chuckles."

"You'll get them." Magic prickled against my skin as I entered. "Protection charm?"

"Of course." She gestured to the plush emerald couch. "Seat?"

"Thanks." I sat and she brought over a tray of tea. I eyed it warily, smiling but not drinking when she handed me a glass.

"Smart," she said.

"Thanks." I pointed to the massive window seat at the front of the house. It'd look right down on the street. "So you like to watch?"

"Of course. Who doesn't?"

"You have a point." Even I liked to spy out my shop window and see what folks were up to. "I have questions about a murder that happened here a couple of hours ago."

"I didn't see the murder, but I saw the cleanup. Vampire Court took care of it."

Disappointment streaked through me. I sank back into the plush couch, suddenly exhausted. I wasn't sure how many more Chuckles I'd be able to conjure at this point. "Were there many of them?"

"Eight." She shuddered. "Powerful, creepy folks."

"I'm trying to find the murderer. Did you overhear anything from the vampires?"

"Nope."

"Do you know anything about the victim? His name was

Marin Olerafort." That was what they'd ask on the TV shows. Find the murderer by learning about the victim.

I so had the hang of this.

The woman held out a hand.

I passed over a package of Chuckles. She tucked it into her impressive cleavage.

"Careful, those could melt in there. Get sticky."

"Maybe that's how I like it." She grinned, revealing a mouth of gold teeth.

I winced. *Know when you're beat.* This lady could out-gross me anyway. She would take this victory.

"You do you." I leaned forward. "What can you tell me about Marin?"

Please know something.

"He worked with vampires. And he liked to visit the woman who lived down the road to the left. Apartment 1B."

"How often?"

"Often enough that you should pay her a visit." She held out a hand, gaze expectant.

I passed the last pack of Chuckles over. She tucked it into her cleavage. *Okay.*

"Is that all you know?"

"About this Marin fellow, yes."

"Thanks." I stood. "Looks like I'm off to find 1B."

"No, you're not."

I stiffened, then tilted my head at her, hoping to give off the look of an angry bird of prey. Not sure I quite nailed it. "I'm not?"

"No. You can't find 1B. It's hidden."

Shit. "Can you help me?"

"For more Chuckles, of course."

I sighed, then called on my magic. A few more packs and I'd be drained. I was good at finding things because of my dragon sense, but I didn't want to risk relying on that alone, since it didn't always work unless I had good info about what I was hunting.

And I *really* needed to find 1B.

I conjured two more packs of Chuckles and handed them over.

She took them, shoved them down the hatch of her bra, then smiled serenely. "You need to seek the everliving vine. It blooms blood red and pricks like a knife."

"Hmmm. Okay." I could work with that. It'd give me something to envision so my dragon sense could latch on. "That all?"

"No. There is no door. Pet a rose petal and say that Clarita sent you. And don't startle her. She is easily spooked."

"Perfect." My favorite kind of person to question.

The woman chuckled and stood, then gestured me to the door. "The Chairman will lead you out."

The big black cat who'd led me here rose from his spot on the rug, then stalked to the door. The Chairman really suited him. I waved to the woman, then followed the Chairman down the stairs and out the main door, which slammed unceremoniously behind me.

In the cold dark of the alley, my newfound clue suddenly seemed small by comparison. But I called upon my dragon sense anyway, feeding it a mental image of the everliving vine with blood red blooms and knife thorns.

It took a moment—an eternity, actually—before my dragon sense clued in. Then it tugged about my middle. *Hard.*

I followed it left, away from Fair Fortune Alley, headed deeper down the narrow street. The moon shined brightly upon the cobblestones that were flecked with snow. More rats streaked along to my left. Good company.

My dragon sense pulled me toward another blank brick wall. This one had no door, but it did have a thick vine crawling up the front. Blood red blooms—like roses on steroids—were nestled amongst the dagger-like thorns.

I *really* wanted to pick one.

That was a terrible freaking idea. Clarita had said to pet a rose petal. I ran a finger down the velvety red surface. "Clarita sent me."

Magic shimmered on the air, and the roses dissolved, followed shortly by the thorns and the vines. A blue door appeared. 1B was painted on the surface in gold.

"Clarita?" the voice asked.

"Yes." I strove to keep my voice calm, so as not to startle her. "She said that I could find you at the everliving vine."

I swore I could hear the annoyed sigh from behind the door. A moment later, it opened to reveal a pretty blonde woman who looked like she ran the PTA. Her eyes were an ice blue that cut right through me, and she was thin enough that a stiff wind could blow her away.

Despite her everyday PTA appearance, there was something weird about her. Just like there had been with Clarita. But I couldn't place it.

"What can I do for you?" Her voice was as cold as her eyes.

I sure hoped she didn't want any Chuckles. "I'm here to ask you about the murder of Marin Olerafort. I understand that you were friends."

Her ice eyes widened at that, and her jaw stiffened. At her side, her hand fisted until the knuckles were white. "I have no idea who you are talking about."

"Of course you know Marin." Shit, was I the first one to tell her that he'd died? "Wait, did you not know about his death?"

Idiot.

"I don't know what you're talking about." Her voice wavered, but it was hard to tell if it was sadness or anger.

"You were friends with Marin. Please, help me. I need to find his killer."

"I'm sorry. I know nothing." She slammed the door shut. It

disappeared and the everliving vine grew up from the pot on the ground.

I stepped back. "Well, shit."

"That's an understatement." The deep voice sounded from behind me.

I jumped a mile into the air. I swear to fate I could see the city below me, spread out as golden lights creeping over the Oregon countryside. When I finally landed, fear sweat had broken out on my palms. Slowly, I turned.

CHAPTER FIVE

The Enforcer stood on the other side of the alley, leaning against a brick wall. Though he was far too big to ever look elegant, he somehow managed it. But it was a lounging jungle cat's I'm-about-to-eat-you elegant. His eyes pierced right through me, and he looked like he was poised to attack. His dark hair swept back from his forehead in the sexiest, most artful disarray I'd ever seen.

Omigod, had I just thought he was sexy?

I was a certifiable idiot. The kind that deserved a plaque on her wall. Or on her tombstone. *Here lies the body of the idiot who was attracted to a killer vampire Enforcer. May she rest in stupidity.*

"Did you think you could outrun me?" he asked.

"Kinda hoped to, at least until I found a clue that proved I was innocent."

"Innocent? You drugged my guards."

"But I didn't kill them. Just like I didn't kill Marin."

He crossed his arms and gave me a skeptical brow raise, then glanced at the wall behind me. "You're trying to prove your innocence?"

"You believe I'm innocent?"

"What I believe is that you are somewhere you shouldn't be, talking to people you shouldn't have the ability to see. Much less talk to."

"I can talk to anyone I want."

The corner of his mouth pulled back in something that was almost a grin but at the same time not even close. "Apparently so."

"I've found a clue, though. So you have to let me go."

"Hardly." He stepped forward.

I backed up. My heart thundered, and sweat broke out on my palms, as if my primitive lizard brain remembered him slapping the collar on me.

"We need to get out of here," he said.

"I'm not going anywhere with you."

"Yes, you are." His gaze fell to the collar. "If you want to keep that head of yours."

"Bastard." Of course I wanted to keep my freaking head.

"Then come on." He held out his hand.

"I'm not holding your hand."

"I'm transporting you, not asking you out. We can't talk here. It's not private."

"My friends are here with me. I can't just ditch them."

"Loyal."

"Like a postcard of a golden retriever."

His brow quirked. "Paul Simon?"

He recognized the lyrics. I wouldn't have pegged that. "Since I'm not a moron, yes."

"That's debatable. Come on. You can call your friends to let them know you've left." He eyed the collar, the threat implicit.

"Fine." I grabbed his palm, both attracted and annoyed.

His strong hand closed around my own. A second later, I was sucked into the ether. It spit us out in the middle of the business district. The tall, darkened buildings glowered down upon us. Most busy bees had gone home for the night.

"Here?" I asked. "You got some banking to do?"

"Smart-ass." But the look in his eyes kinda suggested that he thought I was funny.

Weird. "Give me a moment to call my friends." I pointed to a light post about twenty feet away. "I'm going over there to do it."

"Don't want me eavesdropping?"

"Don't be weird. Of course I don't want you listening to me. I'm going to say terrible things about you."

This time, I'd bet at least seventy-five cents that there was a grin in his gaze.

Nah, that was nuts. I wouldn't even bet a dime.

"Fine. Be quick."

I turned and hurried to the light post, then pressed my fingertips against the comms charm at my neck.

"Guys?" I whispered.

"Yeah?" Cass whispered back.

"I've been nabbed by the Enforcer."

"Damn!" Del hissed.

"My thoughts exactly. He's taken me back to his place in the business district." I didn't need to tell them exactly where to find me. If they needed to, their dragon senses would lead them right to me. "Anyway, I'll be in touch."

"Be safe. We'll keep looking for clues, though we've had no luck yet."

"Thanks, guys. And hey, look after Fabio, okay?"

"Of course," Del said. "I'll drive him like he's my own."

We cut the line, and I returned to the Enforcer. He lounged against a light post, doing another effortless impression of a jaguar that could take my head off.

Not so funny thing was, he could.

"What's your name, anyway?" I asked.

"Ares."

"Like the god of war?"

He shrugged. "If the shoe fits."

"But not like, *the* Ares."

"No, gods are myths."

"Myths can be based on people."

"Well, this one isn't based on me. I'm only twenty-eight, not twenty-eight hundred. Follow me."

He led me toward the front door of the tallest building in Magic's Bend. It held offices as far as I knew, but there was a doorman who looked like he should be standing outside of some fancy apartment building in New York, letting Eloise in and out.

"Sir," the doorman intoned. His face looked like every face I'd ever seen. As boring and bland as wheat bread. It was almost as if he tried to be invisible.

"Jeeves." Ares nodded.

Jeeves held open the door, and I followed Ares into the elegant lobby. I hurried up beside him. "Are you freaking kidding me? The doorman's name is Jeeves? Is he also a butler?"

The corner of Ares's mouth tugged up just slightly, though his eyes remained chilly. "Just a doorman."

"Okay, then." I looked around at the fancy couches and potted plants. "I thought this was an office building."

"The bottom floors are." He pressed the button for the elevator. "The tops floors are apartments, and this is the residential entrance."

"And we couldn't just transport into your house?"

He tossed me an unimpressed glance. "As if I'd allow transporting into my home."

He'd blocked it for security reasons, I guessed. Smart.

He stuck his key into a slot in the elevator, and we rode in silence up to his apartment. The doors opened onto a small, private lobby, and he used his key again to enter his apartment.

I whistled. "Fancy."

The apartment was huge, with high ceilings and a wall of windows looking out onto Magic's Bend. It was modern and beautiful and cold, a bit like the man himself.

I wandered toward the low gray couch. The leather looked soft as silk. It faced a massive marble fireplace.

"You should have a white bearskin rug in front of that fireplace."

"Not my style."

"I imagine not." Too tacky for ol' Ares. "You really live here?"

"Occasionally." He strode to the open kitchen behind a half wall.

"Multiple homes, huh?" I shook my head. "I feel you. They can be a burden."

I so did not have multiple homes, but I wasn't above making fun of him for his.

"Can I get you a drink?" he asked.

"Will it be blood?"

He glanced back at me, brows raised. "Are you offering?"

As fear dampened my palms, I regretted my joke. "Nope. And, uh, I'll just have a water."

He nodded.

I followed him toward the kitchen, veering off to stand at the huge dining room table set into the corner. Windows surrounded it on both sides, providing expansive views out onto the rolling lights of Magic's Bend. The dark patch beyond had to be the sea. Though we were basically a coastal city, I didn't go there often.

Ares joined me, passing me a glass of water. I took it, careful not to touch his hand nor look too directly at him. Not only did he scare me, his beauty kinda blinded me.

I didn't like it. He'd be easier to trust if he were ugly.

But he wasn't. He had the face of a guy who got everything he wanted. And what he wanted right now was to pin a murder on me.

I sipped the water to wet my parched throat. "What are we doing up here?"

"Talking about what you were doing back in Darklane. Returning to the scene of the crime? Did you want a memento?"

"Ugh, no." I set the water on the glass table just a little too hard. Thankfully, nothing cracked. "I was there looking for clues about who actually did it so that you'd take this damned collar off me."

"Did you find one?" he asked.

"Of course. PTA lady has one."

"PTA lady?"

"You know, Parent Teacher Association? She looks all pressed and proper, besides the fact that there is something weird about her."

"Weird? As weird as you being able to walk in the Shadowlands?" He stepped close, his magic pressing in on me. I swore I could feel heat roll off him, though that was crazy.

I stepped back. "What the hell are you talking about?"

He frowned. "Nothing. Tell me what you learned from the PTA woman."

I wanted to know more about these Shadowlands, but now wasn't the time to push. "She knew Marin. And I bet she has a clue about the murder. I just need to figure out what."

"How did you know how to seek her? That seems suspicious that you wandered right to the door of the woman who has a clue."

"Well, you said I wasn't just a Conjurer. I also have a bit of Seeker gift. Not enough that it's worth mentioning, but sometimes it works." Lies. Seekers were harmless Magica who could find things. I could find things because I was a FireSoul. We were not harmless.

"A Seeker? Really?"

"Yeah. My mom's side." Not that I could actually tell him a thing about my mother. I didn't know a thing myself.

"And it led you to her. To a clue that you think will absolve you of the crime?" That skeptical look came back to his face.

"So you trust me? That I didn't do it?"

"I don't trust you. There's something strange about your

magic and you're a suspect. Suspects wear the collar so you don't run for it. In three days, if I'm not convinced you're innocent, you go in front of the Vampire Court for sentencing. Or that collar becomes a real problem for you."

My stomach pitched. "A head-removing problem."

"Exactly."

I scowled. "I won't be running. Is it true that one of your court members can read minds?"

He nodded. "Doyen can. It's annoying."

I swallowed hard. That was bad news for me. "Can she read yours?"

"No longer. I learned to protect my thoughts. But it took a long time."

Shit. I definitely could not end up in front of the Vampire Court. Not if this Doyen could look inside my head and figure out that I was a FireSoul.

I was going to have to help him figure out who the killer was. It was the only way to save my own hide.

"Tell me about the man who was murdered. Was he a vampire?"

"No, but he was a valued ally to the Vampire Court. He was one of our own. We are responsible for him." His hands fisted at his side, and his lips tightened.

Interesting.

If I didn't know better, I'd think he missed Marin. That he'd cared for him. Was he fighting to avenge someone he'd loved? Did the ice man really have feelings?

But I didn't want to explore that right now. Ares wasn't a real person to me. His feelings didn't matter. He was an obstacle I needed to get through to prove my innocence.

"We need to go question that lady," I said. "Or better yet, I need to sneak into that house. Could you distract her while I sneak in? I have an invisibility potion."

He sighed. "I can't say I'm surprised that you want to be involved in this."

"Of course I do. I can't just leave it up to you. I solve my own problems."

"But I don't need your help."

"Sure, you could probably just bust in and search the place, but that's a terrible idea. Loads of supernaturals have spells that quickly dispose of incriminating things. Stealth is always the best way."

He frowned. "You have a point. I wasn't planning to just *bust in*, as you put it. But two will make it go more smoothly."

"Good. I'll do the searching, since I'm good at finding things. You do the distracting. And you are a fresh face who she hasn't seen before. Maybe you'll get more answers than I did.

"That's a good plan." He glanced at his watch. "It's eleven now. We can go back in the morning. It'll be quieter then, anyway."

"In the morning? Aren't you a vampire?"

"Halfbreed. I can walk in the sun."

I shook my head. "There are no halfbreeds. It's impossible. Vampires can't breed outside their species.

"Most can't. My parents were an exception."

"Oh." *Crap.* He could walk in the light? That would make him really strong. And even more dangerous. I hiked a thumb toward the door. "I'll just be seeing myself out, then."

"Absolutely not. You'll sleep in the guest room."

"Here?" My heart raced.

"I'm not letting you out of my sight until this is settled."

"I'm not going to run off." I tapped the collar, my stomach dropping at the feel of the metal. My neck had already gotten used to the weight. I could forget it was there until I touched it. "This will keep me compliant, don't you worry."

"That's fine. But you're staying here."

I scowled at him, but I was beat. As long as I wore this collar, he would win. "Fine. I'll stay here. But you have to feed me."

He nodded once, then turned to the kitchen. I watched him for a moment, trying not to appreciate the view of broad shoulders and a great butt. It wasn't fair that such a jerk was so hot.

"What do you like?" he called.

"Anything with cheese." I followed him into the kitchen, which was a beautiful, modern affair. A bit like cooking in the future would be, I assumed.

"How about a cheese sandwich?" He opened the huge stainless steel fridge.

"As long as you have pickles, that sounds great."

"You're in luck." He pulled out the ingredients, setting them on the white marble counter. In his kitchen, he didn't look like such a killer vampire Enforcer.

He just looked good. And kinda normal.

No! Bad Nix.

I was too old and too smart to fall for a pretty face. And that was all this guy had going for him.

That, and the ability to make a mean cheese sandwich. It only took him a couple minutes, but the final product looked amazing. He didn't skimp on the good stuff.

When he handed the plate over, I took it gratefully. With all the stress, I hadn't eaten in almost twelve hours.

"Mind if I eat this in my room?" I really didn't have any more energy for getting whiplash. Being both attracted to him and scared of him was exhausting.

"Suit yourself." He nodded toward the other end of the apartment. "Down the hall, second door on the left."

"Thanks." I spun and retreated, hurrying across the living room and toward the hallway.

The second door on the left led into a massive bedroom done in about fifty shades of grey.

I winced. *Damn*, that was a bad pun. But it was true.

The room was all gray and all fabulous.

There was a wall of windows providing the most glorious

view out onto Magic's Bend. The city lights glittered in the dark. There was a massive bed and fireplace, with weird-looking furniture that was too modern for my taste.

Fancy, fancy. But still pretty, I had to admit.

I curled up on one of the strange couches and tapped my comms charm.

"Del? Cass?"

"You okay?" Cass asked.

"Yeah."

"He didn't hurt you?" Del asked.

"No. I'm set up with a cheese sandwich in a fabulous suite with a view overlooking Magic's Bend. We're at the top of the biggest building in the business district."

"Nice. So he's loaded?" Cass asked.

"Yeah. Though money can't buy charm." I bit into my sandwich and almost groaned at the amazing taste. Apparently money bought cooking lessons, because this humble sandwich tasted amazing.

"Well, we didn't find any clues," Cass said.

"But we did get Fabio back to your apartment," Del said.

"Thanks." I took another bite.

"What's your plan now?" Del asked.

I told them about our recon plans for the next morning.

"That should be good," Cass said. "Let us know if you need us."

I swallowed the last bite of sandwich. "Will do. Could one of you watch the shop tomorrow?"

"No problem," Del said. "I've got it."

"Thanks, guys. Love you."

"Love you back," they said in unison.

I cut off the comms charm and stared out at Magic's Bend, mulling over my situation. No matter how I looked at it, it wasn't great. But I also wasn't gonna quit.

So there was only one way to go, and that was forward.

~

As it turned out, *forward* meant snooping around the Enforcer's house in the middle of the night. Despite my exhaustion, I couldn't sleep. Not with everything that was going on.

So I crept out of the room around one in the morning and snuck down the hall toward the living room. My heartbeat pounded, echoing in my ears, but it slowed as I got comfortable with sneaking around.

In the living room, the lights had been turned off so that the only illumination came from outside. The floor-to-ceiling windows revealed a gorgeous view of the twinkling yellow lights of Magic's Bend. Kinda made me feel like I was on top of the stars.

Not a bad place to live.

But so barren. I studied the impeccably decorated space. Any clues about Ares would be subtle.

A sleek TV was propped on a table with little doors. I peeked inside the console, but found only a cable box with no DVDs or games or anything. A few paperbacks sat inside—mystery novels.

It seemed that Ares didn't spend a lot of time on leisure activities, unless he had a serious addiction to Netflix.

A small table by the window caught my eye. There were two chairs—one on either side of the table. Like a gaming table. I tiptoed over.

An old chess set was laid out on the beautiful wooden surface. I picked up the king, studying the smoothed sides. It was old and worn down, obviously well loved. From the look of the slightly worn leather on the seats of the chairs on either side of the table, the set was still in use.

But who did Ares play with? He didn't strike me as the kind of guy who had a lot of buddies. He was so professional and to the point. Even his books were kinda like his job. He was solving murder mysteries even in his free time.

And the chess set—that was a strategy game. As one of the three big vamp rulers in charge of all vampire society, strategy would be important to him.

But he definitely lived here for a lot of the time, despite his mysterious multiple houses. The fridge had been well stocked when I'd peeked in, and this place had a lived-in feel despite its spotless perfection.

I left the living room, skipping the kitchen in favor of the hallway on the other side of the apartment. I hadn't been down this hall.

I kept my footsteps silent as I slipped into the first door on the left.

An office.

A massive desk sat in front of the full-length windows. Once again, the light from outside made it unnecessary to turn on the lights. I wouldn't have risked it anyway.

I snuck toward the desk. Opening the drawers seemed risky. That was too invasive, especially if I were caught.

A photo frame on the desk caught my eye. I picked up the heavy silver frame and studied the figures within.

Three people smiled out from the photo. It was formal and posed, but they looked happy enough. Ares, as a child, grinned out at me. No question that it was him. And the man had to be his father. They looked so similar.

Had his father been the Vampire Enforcer before Ares? Was it inherited?

But the woman... She didn't look much like Ares besides the eyes. She was definitely his mom. I angled the photo to get a bit more light on the surface and gasped.

She was wearing the traditional robes of the Order of the Magica. She was part of the Magica government? But married to a vampire?

My skin chilled.

I didn't like how powerful Ares was, but I felt a little better

71

knowing that he was a vampire and part of a government that had nothing to do with Magica. Had he been a member of my own government….

That'd be way scarier.

But his mom was?

"What are you doing?" Ares's ice-cold voice made me jerk my head up. His eyes were just as chilly.

The vampire was *mad.*

"You're snooping," he said. "For what?"

"I wanted to know more about you."

He strode over, every muscle tense. I set the photo down on the desk, swallowing hard and stepping back. He crowded me against the window, not touching me, but close enough that I could feel the heat of him.

"You're not even going to pretend you were lost?" he said. "Couldn't sleep?"

"That second part is true, but nope. I just wanted to know more about you."

He frowned. "Do *not* do that again."

My heart thundered, but I straightened. "You're just going to have to sleep with one eye open. Because as long as I've got this collar on, I'm going to go after whatever information I think will help me." And my *deirfiúr.* If I ended up in front of the Vampire Court and Doyen could read in my mind that they were also FireSouls…

"And knowing about me will help you?" he demanded.

"Why not? Helps to know your jailor."

"I'm not your jailor."

I touched the collar at my neck. "This begs to differ."

"But you're not scared of me."

"Nope. I'm scared of this collar, but not of you." That was slightly a lie, but he seemed to like that I was tough. I nodded toward the desk behind him. "Your mom is a Magica?"

He stepped back, giving me a bit of room to breathe. "I said I was a half breed."

"Yeah, but I didn't know what kind. What is she?"

"A variety of things. Those gifts were passed down to me."

So she'd been powerful. Which made him powerful, too, as well as being a vampire. "What kind of magic did she pass down to you?"

"You'll just have to wait and see."

"Hmmm. And she's an Order member?"

"Was." His gaze turned dark. "They're both dead now."

"I'm sorry." My chest ached for him. I knew what it felt like to not have parents.

"So am I."

"What did she do at the Order?"

"She led the special commission to hunt FireSouls. She felt that she was protecting the people with her work."

My breath caught, and my head spun. I finally managed to squeak out, "Oh. Interesting."

Holy crap. He'd been born with a mom who hunted my kind. Chills raced over my skin.

"Are you all right?" he asked.

"Fine." I smiled, hoping it was convincing. "I'm going to just hit the hay though, okay? Long day."

He stared hard at me, trying to read something on my face. I gave him nothing. Finally, he nodded, but there was something in his eyes. It looked a hell of a lot like suspicion. My skin prickled.

"Okay. But no more snooping." His voice was hard.

Relief loosened my tensed shoulders. He was still suspicious—it was clear in his eyes and the set of his mouth—but he'd given me an out.

"No problem." I skirted around him, my palms damp, and left the room.

As I hurried down the hall, I couldn't help but feel like I'd made a very narrow escape.

CHAPTER SIX

The next morning, after a shower in the massive marble room he called a guest bathroom, I found Ares in the kitchen.

He was drinking a cup of coffee, though I kinda wished it had been blood. That, at least, would have grossed me out. I didn't like thinking that he was sexy and scary at the same time. I was a more straightforward kind of girl.

"Sleep well?" he asked.

"Surprisingly well, considering that I'm wearing a murder collar."

His expression didn't change. Ice man. "There's coffee if you want some. And muffins."

"Thanks." I helped myself to some coffee and a muffin, then turned to him. "So you'll just zap us there after breakfast?"

"That's the plan.

"A-plus." I sipped the coffee, which bore a remarkable resemblance to rocket fuel. I liked it.

We finished breakfast quickly, then he took my hand and transported us to the main road in Darklane. Though the sun had been bright outside my bedroom window, it was a dreary morning here in Darklane. But it was almost always dreary here, as if the dark magic blocked out some of the sunlight.

The street was dead silent, like the whole neighborhood was sleeping off the night before.

"Ready?" he asked.

"Like a cat's ready for tuna."

I followed him toward Fair Fortune Alley. He entered a few steps ahead of me, then turned to watch me.

"Whatcha lookin' at, champ?" My bravado faded when I entered the alley. It was darker in here. Even darker than out on the main alley. "This is the Shadowlands, isn't it? That's why it's darker."

"Maybe." His gaze raked me. "Did you feel anything strange when you entered? An aversion to this place?"

"I always have an aversion to Darklane." Understanding dawned. "You transported us to the main road so you could watch me enter Fair Fortune Alley. It was a test of some kind."

He shrugged.

"Did I pass?"

"I have no idea." He turned and started down the alley. "We'll discuss it later."

I hurried to catch up. We didn't see a soul as we made our way to the PTA lady's house—not even the rats. Even they had to sleep off the night before. Right before we turned onto her road, I stopped him.

"I'm going to take the potion now." I dug the little vial out of my pocket and chugged it down. Mud. Ack. A chill shivered over my skin as it went to work, turning me entirely invisible.

"That's fast acting," he said.

"Connor's the best. Now lead the way."

I followed him toward PTA lady's street. When we reached the everliving vine, he stroked the petal with one finger. Had he been spying on me long enough yesterday to learn that trick from me?

The vine faded into nothing, and the blue door appeared. Ares knocked. I sidled up to the wall near the door, ready to creep in when I got an opening.

"By order of the Vampire Court, I command you to open this door." Ares's voice had a chill that I recognized from our first meeting.

I shivered.

After a few moments, the door finally creaked open. PTA lady was well-pressed again—not a hair out of place—but her face told a different story.

Her icy eyes widened at the sight of Ares. She gasped. "Enforcer!"

"I have some questions for you regarding the death of Marin Olerafort."

Her mouth opened and closed like she was a goldfish. The wheels were clearly turning in her head. To lie or not to lie? She shifted left just enough to provide me with an in, so I slipped into her house and left Ares to handle her.

She might look like the president of the PTA, but her house sure didn't. It was dark and creepy as a fictional witch's evil lair. The walls were painted black, and the lights were dim. Black lace abounded. Curtains, tablecloths, doilies.

I shivered, creeping along the hall, using my dragon sense to lead me toward a possible clue. There was something in the back of the house and high up, maybe on a third floor. I just had to find it.

I passed a formal dining room and a living room. The living room had the TV blaring to some horrible morning show, and a terrier snoozed on the black couch. The little gray dog perked up when I passed.

Shit. He could smell or hear me. Or both.

And he was interested. He hopped down off the sofa and trotted toward me. The last thing I needed was for him to start barking.

Quickly, I conjured a steak and tossed it to him. He caught it out of the air and chomped down, no longer interested in me.

Thank fates he wasn't a good guard dog.

A narrow staircase at the end of the hall led me up two stories to the third floor. The air felt stale and abandoned up here, but my quarry was farther up. I hurried toward the end of the hall, aware that Ares could only ask questions for so long.

A cord dangled from the ceiling.

Jackpot.

I tugged on the cord, wincing when the wooden ladder descended with a loud creaking sound. I didn't hesitate—no time to waste now—and scrambled up into the attic. It was dark, with just a watery stream of light filtering into the room. The whole place was full of crap—but it was a particularly large pile of junk that called to me.

I dug through it, finally finding a box on the floor. It was the size of a shoebox, but made of fancy wood with mother-of-pearl inlays. My dragon sense tugged hard.

This was definitely it.

I eased the lid open, disappointed when I saw only a couple photos.

Dang.

But it was still the thing I sought—my dragon sense was certain. I picked up the photos, and something gold flashed in the bottom of the box.

Hey. Now this was cool.

I picked it up. It was heavy, with engravings on both sides. Whatever this was, it was important. I shoved it in my pocket, then pulled out my cell phone and snapped pics of the two photos. At a glance, it was clearly PTA lady and Marin in their younger years. Both wore the medallion proudly around their necks.

Though I was tempted to take the originals to help prove my point, this box had sentimentality written all over it.

It was important to PTA lady. I couldn't just yank the photos. Especially when my camera shots would do just as well to prove my point. And if I had a chance, I'd return the medallion once we'd figured out if it could help us.

Finished, I snapped the box shut and tucked it back under the pile of junk, then hurried from the attic. I raced down the hall as silently as I could, then down the stairs and toward the front door.

PTA lady was still talking to Ares, but she was clearly annoyed by now. Her shoulders were stiff, and her magic fizzed around her. It felt like carbonated water on my tongue. Weird.

Right before I passed the living room, I conjured another steak and tossed it to the schnauzer who waited for me. This time, though, he ignored the meat and tilted his head to study me. Though he couldn't see me, he could clearly smell me.

Damn it. I'd given him too much before.

He yipped, a high pitch alert that echoed in the hall.

Double damn.

PTA lady turned, her icy eyes wide.

"Who's there?" she barked.

The hall was long, and I was still about fifteen feet from the exit. In a half second, her magic swelled.

Shit.

Quickly, I conjured a shield. I didn't know what she'd try throwing at me, but she was clearly pissed. Her eyes were wide and angry as she hurled a blast of energy in my direction. I heaved my shield up in front of my face. The magic slammed into the metal.

I stumbled, going to my knees, then clambered up, careful to keep the shield in front of me.

She threw another blast, which slammed me into the wall. Pain sang through my back. PTA lady yelped. I peeked over my shield as I raced down the hall toward the exit.

Ares had wrapped his arms around her chest and neck. His eyes flared silver and bright, and his fangs—which I hadn't seen before now—lengthened into sharp white points.

Oh shit, I hoped he wouldn't bite her.

Instead, he pressed his hands against a spot on her neck, and her eyes rolled up in her head. She collapsed against him. He stepped into the house with her in his arms.

Still invisible, I slipped by them and out into the cool winter air. I glanced behind me.

Gently, Ares laid her on the ground in the hall then stepped out into the cool air and shut the door behind him.

"Where are you?" he asked.

"Here." I reached out to touch his arm.

He turned toward me, then wrapped an arm around my waist and pulled me to him. The warm strength of his chest made the air rush from my lungs. I shifted the shield that I still held and shivered as he enfolded me in both arms. In a flash, he transported us away from PTA lady's house.

A moment later, we appeared on the main street in Darklane. It was past ten, but the place felt as sleepy as it would have at six a.m. The only person awake was a man leaning out the third story window of ramshackle old Victorian house. He wore a stocking cap, and the whole thing looked like something out of a dark fairytale.

"Are you okay?" Ares's concerned gaze searched the area near my head, though he was still slightly off.

He was worried about me?

It was hard to tell, from the firm set of his jaw and his usually cold gaze. But there was just the tiniest hint of worry that shone through his eyes.

I pulled away from him. "I'm fine. I'll be visible soon. I didn't take much of the potion."

"Did you get what you were looking for?"

"I think so." My dragon sense certainly thought so. Since the medallion was stuffed in my pocket, it was invisible along with me.

Fortunately, I felt the magic prickle along my skin.

"You're becoming visible," he said.

I glanced down at my arm. Yep. "Come on, let's find some place quieter."

We moved from the main sidewalk to a little shadowed alley and tucked ourselves into the entrance. We turned our backs to the main street. I set the shield down against the alley. It was too heavy to carry around, and someone here would find it and make use of it.

Standing like this, I was pressed up close enough that I could smell his subtle, masculine scent. I could no longer smell his magic because he had his signature repressed, but the scent of him alone was enough to make my head spin.

"Well?" he asked.

"Hang on." I took the medallion from my pocket and handed it over. As he inspected it, I pulled up the photos on my cell phone and held it up. "These too. There were two photos of Marin and PTA lady together, back when they were younger."

Ares looked up from his inspection of the golden medallion and studied the photo.

"They're wearing this medallion in that photo." He pointed. "It's peeking out from behind their scarves."

"We need to figure out what this medallion is."

"I can send pictures to Dr. Garriso. He's a scholar at the Museum of Magical History and knows almost everything."

"Fine." He held up the medallion so I could snap a photo of each side.

A few moments later, I'd sent the pictures and a text that read. *Recognize this?*

"Let's just see," I said.

It took only a moment to hear back. *I will consult my sources but it will take time. Any more info would be helpful.*

I showed it to Ares. "Not great."

"No. You don't have a lot of time."

I scowled at him. Forget my fantasy that I'd seen concern on his face earlier. "You're a jerk."

"It's the truth. I need concrete evidence for the Vampire Court before that collar can be removed."

A rock suddenly appeared in my throat. "You mean, you don't have the power to remove it?"

"No. I am one of three. Without them, it cannot be removed. They will only believe hard evidence of your innocence."

Breathing was suddenly a bit more difficult. It was hard enough to know that he held my life in his hands. But it was actually two other unknown vampires?

Shit. "Well, then we need answers about this damned medallion."

"I have someone who might be able to help. We can go see him now."

I grabbed onto that like the lifeline it was. "Good. Where do they live?"

"Down the street. At the edge of Fair Fortune Alley."

"Lead on."

We hurried down the street. Here in Darklane, the air always smelled a tiny bit rotten. Dark magic. We passed a few folks going about their business. One woman looked like a fairytale witch, complete with black robes and pointed hat.

"We're here." Ares pointed to a big green door with the number 13 painted in silver. The windows on either side had the shutters closed tight against any light. Ares stepped onto the stoop and knocked.

"Who is it?" A creaky voice filtered through the thick wooden door.

"Ares. Open up, Laphraig."

"Of course." The voice suddenly sounded a lot more conciliatory, and the door opened.

Apparently Ares's name commanded respect. Or at least obedience.

The man who stood in the doorway looked like a skeleton. His cheekbones were sharp as glass, his neck a toothpick. He was easily as tall as Ares but half the weight. From the opulence of the hallway behind him—which was paneled in green silk with glittering crystal chandeliers—his slenderness was more choice than necessity.

In his sharply pressed black suit and flat-topped hat, he looked like one of the judgmental puritan preachers from any of the movie versions of *The Legend of Sleepy Hollow.*

Even his dark green eyes blazed with the light of a fanatic.

I shivered. It took a lot to make me nervous—like the deadly vampire Enforcer standing next to me. But this guy? Laphraig? He was scary.

"How can I be of assistance?" Laphraig's voice was just as creaky and whispery as it had been through the door.

"We have something we would like you to read," Ares said.

Laphraig gave a small bow and stepped back. I followed Ares into the house.

"The sitting room, if you please," Laphraig said.

Ares led the way down the darkly luxurious hallway to a sitting room on the left. This, too, was done entirely in shades of dark green. The furniture was old and fancy and reminded me a bit of the sitting rooms in *Pride and Prejudice.* The movie version, of course.

A small black dog sat on a chair. He was as plump as his master was skinny.

Ares turned to me. "The medallion?"

I took it from my pocket and held it out for Laphraig. He approached, reaching out a skeletal hand. Just as his fingertips touched it, he stiffened.

His nostrils flared, and he looked at me, his green eyes bright. "What are you?" he asked.

"None of your business." I shoved the medallion at him. "Do your thing."

He stepped closer, his gaze riveted to me. His breath was coming a bit quicker now as well. He licked his lips. I could *feel* the hunger coming off him.

I shuddered.

"So long. It's been so long," he muttered to himself.

"Laphraig!" Ares barked.

Laphraig straightened and stepped back, taking the medallion with him. He scuttled away to the corner, turning his back to us.

What the hell? I mouthed at Ares.

Instead of commiserating with me, he gave me an interested look. As if he were trying to figure out what Laphraig saw in me.

I scowled at him.

Laphraig hunched over the medallion in the corner for a while, then turned back to us, his eyes bright. "Secrecy shrouds this medallion."

"That's our problem," I said.

"Yes. But I mean that this charm represents Secrecy. Or a secret society. It is shrouded in mystery the likes of which I have never seen."

"Huh." I had no idea if that was helpful. I looked at Ares. "What do you think?"

"No idea." He pinned Laphraig with a hard stare. "Is that all you've got?"

"Yes. But it's not as little as it seems." He crossed the room toward us, reminding me of a granddaddy longlegs. "It may represent or hold secrets of some kind. Or be a token of membership to an organization."

"That sounds promising," I said.

Laphraig's green eyes snapped to mine, burning with a fiery hunger. He licked his lips. "Yes, girl. Yes. It is. Just like you are."

He moved like Ares, speed incarnate. In the flash of an eye, he was at my throat.

Laphraig's skeletal hands wrapped around my shoulders as his head reared back. Long fangs descended from his mouth.

Vampire!

CHAPTER SEVEN

My heart leapt into my throat. I kneed him in the balls, then delivered a quick punch to the throat. He collapsed backward with a keening cry.

Ares was on him a second later, hauling him upright by the back of his coat. The skeletal vampire shrieked and hissed, clawing for me.

"You think you can bite me?" I conjured a bat and swung it at his head, pulling back on my strength at the last minute.

Didn't want to kill him, after all—even if he had been going for my throat.

The bat collided with his skull, not hard enough to crack it but enough to knock him out. I was a pro, after all.

Ares let go of his jacket, letting Laphraig collapse in a pile.

The little black dog yipped, leapt off the chair, and trotted to his master.

Ares crouched and pressed a hand to Laphraig's throat.

"I didn't kill him." I nudged the body with my boot. "Didn't even crack his skull. He'll just be out a short while."

"Nicely done." Ares grabbed the medallion and stood.

"What the hell was that all about?"

"Let's get out of here, and we can talk about it."

We hurried from the house. I couldn't get out of here quickly enough. Even the air in here gave me the willies. The rank smell of Darklane was a blessing compared to this. When we got outside, I sucked it in, inhaling deep.

"I'm ready to be out of Darklane," Ares said. "You?"

"Totally."

He held out a hand, and I grabbed it, trying not to think of how strong and warm it was. The ether sucked us in, transporting us across town to the historic district.

It was busier here, the lunch hour drawing crowds from the nearby business district. The colorful old buildings contained enough restaurants to feed everyone in Magic's Bend, and it seemed that everyone had showed up to eat.

I stepped away from him.

"Let's get out of the crowd," Ares said. "Come on."

He led me to a restaurant on the bottom floor of a blue Victorian house. A hoity-toity fae with shimmery silver wings opened the door and gestured us inside. The interior was done up in linens and silver. Each of the house's original rooms had been done up in a different color with a few tables.

The fae gestured us through the larger rooms to a small, private one in the back. We sat at the table, and I watched the fae depart, shutting the door behind him.

"You like it fancy," I murmured.

"You could use a good meal. And they're discreet here. Every other place will be full on an afternoon like today."

"Good point."

Our fae waitress returned and took our orders—lobster mac and cheese for me, because I could be fancy too—then disappeared quickly.

I sent Dr. Garriso a new text with the information we'd

learned, then looked up at Ares. He was studying me intently, like I was a bug under a microscope.

He definitely thought there was something weird about me.

And that was bad freaking news.

I shoved aside my nerves. "What the hell was that back there? Laphraig was a vampire?"

"We're not always obvious."

"I know that. But he had some serious blood lust going on." Normally, vampires blended with society unless they had a bad case of blood lust. Outsiders didn't know how they got it—I wasn't sure that even vampires knew—but Laphraig had had a serious case.

"Laphraig has been abstaining." Ares looked pale at the thought.

"From blood?"

"Yes. That's why he's so skinny. But something about you...."

"I eat a diet high in saturated fats?" Cheese mostly. "Perhaps I'm extra tasty?"

"No. That's not it. There's something about you."

"My love of cheddar and mean ability to swing a bat?"

The corner of his mouth cracked up in a smile. "No."

"Then I've got no idea."

"Neither do I. But you can walk in the Shadowlands."

"Which are?" I heaved a sigh. "You vampires are so damned secretive."

"It works for us." Ares leaned back. "Vampires live in another realm, as most people know."

"Yeah, it's why we rarely see you."

"Exactly. Otherwise, you'd hunt us. Only somewhat effectively."

I couldn't imagine anyone effectively hunting and catching him, so I had to agree. But..."You make us into food, so of course we're nervous."

"That's in the past. We only drink from willing victims now."

"Willing? Why would anyone be willing?"

He raised a brow, and the look was devastatingly sexy. Understanding dawned. I'd heard rumors that the bite could be pleasant, but it must have been true.

"Uh, okay, I get it." I checked my phone to see if Dr. Garriso had replied, but he hadn't found anything yet. "So what are the Shadowlands?"

"It's an intermediate point between our realm and yours. It's where the magic from our world seeps into yours and creates a place that is a little bit of both."

"And your world is always in the dark, which is why the shadow lands are darker than the rest of Darklane."

"Exactly. Only vampires and our allies can walk there."

"I'm not your ally."

"Exactly. Which is why you're ability to go there is so interesting."

Time to change the subject. "Marin could go there, but he's not one of you."

"He is our ally though. He worked for us occasionally, finding information. But he had his own life too."

"A life that got him killed."

Ares nodded, his green gaze darkening. "Yes. His secrets got him killed. Secrets have a way of doing that."

I swallowed hard, trying to keep my expression neutral. I was the queen of secrets. An enigma wrapped in a riddle wrapped in mysterious whatever-the-hell. And I didn't want Ares figuring me out. Hell, even *I* hadn't fully figured me out yet. I certainly didn't want Ares to know more about me.

"What are your secrets, Nix?"

"Don't know what you're talking about."

He shrugged. "It's all right. The Court can get them from you."

The food arrived then, carried by two identical fae. They dropped it off quickly and discreetly, then disappeared. Once again, Ares had no blood with his meal. Just a steak and some vegetables. So when *did* he drink blood?

I was so stressed over his previous line of questioning that I had to force down a bite of my mac and cheese. It was so dang good that I almost rolled my eyes. After swallowing, I asked, "So what exactly is the Vampire Court?"

If they were going to get all my secrets, I wanted to know everything I could about them.

He swallowed his bite of steak and said, "There are three branches. Knowledge, Legislation, Law. I am Law."

"What exactly does that mean? You're the warrior?"

"Yes. I protect us from threats. Most of that is by leading the vampire enforcement team. Because I can walk in the sun, I'm perfect for it."

"So you don't spend a lot of time in the Court."

"I'd rather be on the hunt, so it works for me." He grinned, deadly and beautiful.

I shoved a bite of mac and cheese in my mouth, disgusted by my hormones. I was like a freaking teenage boy.

"It must pay well," I said. His house and this restaurant were testament to that.

"I'm one third of the government. I would hope it pays well."

My phone buzzed. I grabbed for it, pressing it to my ear.

"Nix? It's Dr. Garriso." His creaky old voice sent an image of him right into my mind. He was about my height, with wild white hair and a serious English professor vibe. He spent his life in a book-filled office that smelled of books and wore tweed coats with patches on the arms.

He'd helped us with problems before. Beneath the table, I crossed my fingers, hoping he'd be able to help us this time as well.

"Hi, Dr. Garriso. Did you get anything?"

"Of course I did. Just needed a bit more to go on to speed up the process."

89

"What'd you find?"

"Nothing in my sources, but a friend was able to provide me with an address."

"Where to?"

"London. 42 Florence Avenue. It's in a supernatural neighborhood, so you shouldn't have to lie too low."

"Thank you. You're a lifesaver."

"Anytime, my dear, anytime."

I hung up and relayed the information to Ares.

"Just an address?" he said.

"It's more than we had."

"True. And you think this might lead us to the killer?"

I shrugged. "He was murdered right near PTA lady's house. Probably right after visiting her. Now we learn that there is a location that somehow relates to a medallion that is shrouded in secret?"

"Fine. It seems like a good clue."

It had better be, because I'd already lost more than eighteen hours of my allotted seventy-two.

I polished off the last few bites of my pasta, then looked up at him. "I'm going to go call my friends—let them know what I'm doing."

"Must you?"

"Always." I stood. "Meet you out front."

I hurried from the restaurant, igniting the magic in my comms charm as soon as I stepped onto the street. It didn't take long to let them know where I was headed, and by the time I was done, Ares had joined me.

"Ready?" he asked.

"Yep. You can zap us right there?"

He nodded and held out a hand. I took it, and the ether sucked us in, transporting us to a busy street in the middle of London. Fortunately, because this was a neighborhood occupied entirely by supernaturals, we didn't have to worry about humans seeing us appear out of thin air. They'd never enter this part of town because magical spells would drive them away.

It was dark because of the time change, with the evening lights setting the place ablaze. In front of us, an enormous red brick building took up an entire block. A huge clock tower sat atop it, also built of red brick with a pointed black slate roof.

"Twenty bucks that is our destination," I said.

"Agreed," Ares said. "St. Pancras station. Not a very quiet place."

"No, it's really not." I'd seen a program on TV saying it was one of the busiest train stations in London. It was historic, with a glass-roofed atrium housing shops and restaurants and all the hustle and bustle a city like London could provide.

"What do you say we do some recon?" Ares said.

"You read my mind."

We crossed the busy street and climbed the wide steps to a raised stone platform that led to the clock tower. It was about the size of a football field, but there were only a few people standing on it and snapping pictures.

As subtly as I could, I fed my dragon sense my desire to find a clue about the medallion. I made dead certain that my magic didn't flare up—no need to point a flashing arrow at my abilities.

Ares had his head tilted back and was studying the clock tower when I finally got a tug of recognition.

That clock tower was definitely our goal. But how to get in?

"Let's poke around the sides," I said. "Maybe there will be an entrance."

"To where?"

"The clock tower, of course. Something that big and impressive has to be important." *Please buy that load of bull.*

He gave me a skeptical look, but nodded, then held out his hand.

"We can just walk," I said.

"And we're going to. But if we pretend to be a couple, we'll draw less notice."

He did have a point. This was a slightly more touristy part of London, given that it was the entrance and exit hub for any supernaturals who didn't have the ability to transport. Weres and witches and fae who were on vacation were spilling out of the train station behind the clock tower, looking all around and ready to start their travels.

"Fine, good idea." I grabbed his hand.

He grinned. "Try to look like you like me."

"Don't ask the impossible."

He chuckled, and we started off across the flagstones and went down the stairs on the other side of the building. There was a darker side street running alongside the station here. There were no tourists exiting the station on this side, just an alley full of dumpsters and the smell of vomit.

I pointed to it. "That has potential."

"It does."

We turned down the alley. The smell was strong. My head went foggy and weird, as if my brain were swimming in pudding. That was weird. Could it be a spell?

The sight of the spilled garbage sent the worry from my mind. Why hadn't anyone cleaned this up?

Jeez, I hoped my own place wasn't so gross. What if it was? I'd die of embarrassment. I really needed to go clean my house.

Actually, had I left the oven on? I totally had. Oh my god, my house was going to burn down.

I stopped, which made my head spin a bit, and pulled on Ares's hand. It didn't take much. He seemed as anxious to go as I was, his gaze twitchy. I'd bet his house was a mess too. We really needed to get out of here before roaches and rats overran our homes. Or they burned down.

My dragon sense tugged me toward the clock tower, as if trying to remind me of my goal.

Hang on. I shook my head, trying to clear the brain fog.

I almost never used my oven. Once in a blue moon. There was no way it was left on. And no way I'd be afraid of that. Or of my messy house. And Ares's place certainly wasn't dirty.

"There's a repelling enchantment," I said.

"Yes." His brow was creased with concentration as he tried to fight the spell. "We need to keep going."

"Agreed."

We turned back to the alley and pushed through the extreme unease. These were great repelling charms. They attracted almost no attention and would likely drive off anyone who would trespass.

But I had my dragon sense to remind me of the goal. Also, I would never fall for that oven bit.

Eventually, the feeling faded as we crept by dumpsters and piles of trash, which I now realized were an illusion to make the alley look disused. The stink was from the dark magic that protected the alley.

We were about thirty feet in when tiny beestings burst over every inch of my skin. I halted and pulled back until they stopped. Ares followed, his gaze grim.

The beestings were just a warning.

"Protection charms," Ares said.

"Yep." There'd be something worse up ahead. I rubbed my arms to soothe the prickly ache. "But we're definitely onto something."

Ares studied the alley that we had yet to traverse. It was dark and narrow.

"Can you transport us down a ways?" I asked.

His magic flared briefly, bringing with it the taste of whiskey and the feel of a caress against my skin.

He shook his head. "No. Warded from transporting."

No surprise.

"Then let's keep going."

93

We continued walking, fighting our way past the beestings until a thick vine extended out from the wall like an octopus arm. It struck out toward us.

We dived, skidding along the pavement.

Another vine struck out, this one with thorns. The brick walls had been barren until now, but we'd clearly triggered something.

I called upon my magic, conjuring a sword. "Need one?"

"No." Ares jumped up and went for a vine, moving so quickly he could grab it with his bare hands and tear it apart.

I swung my sword, chopping off a vine as it went for my legs. Another hit me in the back, slamming me forward. I rolled, popping up and turning around in time to slice the vine in two. Beside me, Ares was tearing the vines apart as they struck out for me.

We made our way slowly down the alley until the vines stopped coming.

"Pretty good secur—" I started.

My words were cut off by the thunder of footsteps. Demons poured out of a doorway about ten feet down the alley. There were a dozen at least, all dressed in identical black uniforms. They were at least six and a half feet tall with gray skin and sawed-off horns.

Security demons.

Ares charged them. He slashed out with his hand, striking the neck of the closest demon. Blood sprayed, courtesy of the infamous vampire claws that I'd never seen. Vampires shifted physically when in fight mode. Their eyes turned silver and they grew claws while their fangs extended. Though they didn't get any bigger, they became stronger.

A demon charged me, his massive blade raised. I dodged his first blow, plunging my blade into his gut. He roared. I kicked him backward, then swung for the next demon.

My blade sliced across his throat, but not quickly enough. His buddy landed a knife blow to my shoulder before I could swing at him.

Pain flared from the wound as my blood poured free. I kicked the attacking demon in the stomach, then plunged my blade into his throat.

Beside me, Ares had taken out seven demons and was demolishing the eighth with a black sword made of shadow. It was odd looking. He had a cut on his chest, but otherwise looked to be okay.

I turned for the last one, my wounded arm blazing with pain. He swung his sword. I dodged it by a hair's breadth, sucking in my stomach to get that last extra inch, then aimed my blade for his throat.

He was fast, darting out of the way just in time. I lunged for him, sinking my blade into his gut as his sword came at me from the left.

I jumped out of the way, but took a small slice to my side. It still hurt like the devil.

He collapsed. Demon bodies were scattered around us like broken dolls. My wounds sang with pain, and my breaths came like a freight train.

"That was fun," I said.

Ares turned to face me, his gaze blazing from the fight. He opened his mouth, but his eyes widened on something over my shoulder.

I spun.

A mass of demon guards came hurtling toward us. There had to be at least two dozen. Maybe more.

I looked back at Ares. "Time to run."

He nodded, gaze certain. There was no way we could fight that many.

Ares flicked his shadow sword and it disappeared, then he took off. We raced down the alley, back the way we'd come. The pain from my wounds faded as my aching lungs distracted me.

Breath heaving, I glanced back over my shoulder. Ares kept behind me, which was weird, since he was faster. But I only had eyes for the demons.

They were following us, and were only about thirty feet behind.

We had to make it to the main street. They wouldn't come out there—they wouldn't want to be seen. Right?

This seemed like a pretty secret operation—whatever it was—so I freaking hoped I was right.

We sprinted by the fake dumpsters and spilled out onto the main street. I didn't look back—just kept running.

Better safe than sorry.

I raced in front of the oncoming cars, their bright headlights nearly blinding me. Horns blared and brakes screeched.

We reached the other side and pulled to a halt. I spun to check out the demons.

They hadn't followed us out into the street, thank fates.

But people were staring at us. They might be supernaturals and fights might be pretty common among our kind, but we'd still caused a serious traffic disruption and were streaked liberally with blood.

"That went well." I pressed a hand to my chest, panting. More jogging for me.

Ares chuckled, his gaze bright with the thrill of the chase. "Not sure I'd say that."

"We're alive, aren't we?"

"Fair enough. That is a win." His gaze went straight to my wounded side and arm. "You're hurt."

"Just a flesh wound." I raised it to inspect the damage. Pain flared, a lightning bolt of agony through my bicep. Blood had soaked my sleeve and dripped to the pavement. My head spun, and I stumbled slightly. "Bit of blood loss, maybe."

"Maybe."

I tilted to the side, and he swept me up in his arms.

96

"Hey, lemme go." I shoved at him.

"Not a chance in hell. You can't stand."

"Sure I can—" My head spun like my brain was on a carnival ride and had asked for the extra-fast setting. Adrenaline had pushed the pain to the back of my mind, but now...

Now I was about two seconds from passing out if I kept standing.

"Okay," I slurred. "Maybe the cut is deep."

Maaaaybe I could walk under my own steam. But maybe not. And right now, with his strong arms wrapped around me and my head feeling fuzzy, this seemed like a pretty good deal.

No one ever said I was stupid.

If a hot dude wanted to give you a ride, why say no?

Shit. That had a double meaning.

I grimaced. Good thing I hadn't said that aloud.

He gripped me close to him and strode down the sidewalk. I kept my mouth shut.

After a few moments, he turned right and climbed the stairs to a beautiful stone building.

The Pancras Hotel.

"We're getting a hotel?" I asked.

"Yes. It's convenient." The wide glass doors opened automatically, and he strode through.

I looked down at the blood soaking my arm and side, then at the blood staining the front of his shirt. We weren't really dressed for a hotel. And certainly not one as fancy as this.

The lobby was massive and done in shades of pale gold. The furniture looked expensive, and the chandeliers were the size of Fabio. This place was fancy with a capital F.

From behind the mahogany desk, the clerk glared at me, his upper lip curled.

Uh-oh.

We were going to get the boot.

I recognized that look from my days as a teenager on the run with Del and Cass. It wasn't always easy back then to hide our shitty circumstances. People didn't usually like desperate teenagers hanging around their establishments.

Annoyance streaked through me. This guy was just a dick.

His gaze darted up to Ares, then widened.

Ares strode to the desk.

"I'm Ares Warhaven. We need a room."

Recognition dawned in the clerk's muddy eyes. "Of—of course, sir."

There was so much bowing and scraping in his tone that I expected him to curtsey.

Apparently being Ares commanded a lot of fearful resect.

"Make sure it has a view of Saint Pancras station." Ares's voice was entirely without inflection. It was neither haughty nor friendly. This must be his Enforcer In Public voice.

"Then penthouse?" the clerk asked.

"That's fine."

The clerk passed a key over the desk. "I will bill the Vampire Court. Just let us know if we can send anything to the room."

Ares nodded and took the key, then strode away.

"Must be convenient to be you," I said.

"There are perks."

Ares stepped into a ritzy elevator that was big enough to hold a football team, and pressed the button for the top floor.

"How did he know how to bill you?" I asked.

"The Vampire Court travels. We prefer nice hotels and are known among the staff. It's just happy coincidence that this one is located across from the station."

He stayed in this kind of place frequently? Though there was a certain elegance to his features and his walk, he was too big and too deadly-looking to ever fit in in a place like this.

But then, I'd never cared about fitting in, so why should he?

The elevator stopped on the top floor, and Ares carried me out, then found our room at the end of the hall. He slipped the key into the lock, then pushed the door open. It was a large, two-bedroom suite. Wide windows gave an excellent view of the clock tower.

"Good choice." It was suddenly clear why we were staying here.

"I thought so." He set me down on a wide chair in front of the windows, then knelt at my side, inspecting the wound in my arm. His eyes dilated slightly, and his lips parted. The scent of his magic flared. For some reason, it made me think of arousal.

Oh boy. He *really* liked the look of my blood.

I swallowed hard. "You're not going to make a meal of me, right?"'

"No." But hunger was bright in his eyes, and he licked his lips, clearly unconscious of the motion. "Willing donors only, remember?"

"I'm not willing. Just laying that out there. Gotta have good boundaries, right?"

"Yes. Good boundaries. But this cut looks bad."

"It's fine, really."

"You're pale as a sheet and sweaty."

"That run was a good workout."

Carefully, he eased me out of my jacket to inspect the cut more fully. Pain sliced through me and I winced.

"You also have a cut that's almost to the bone," he said. "You're in bad shape."

"The wheezing I was doing while we ran should have told you that."

The corner of his full lips cocked up in a half smile. "You know what I mean."

Gently, he pushed the side of my jacket back to inspect the cut at my waist. "This one isn't as bad, but it's still ugly."

"So's your face." Oh fates, I was a child.

"No, it's not."

I laughed. I might be ridiculous from blood loss and fear, but it didn't seem to bother him.

"You were tough back there," he said.

"It's kinda my job."

"Fighting demons?"

"Protecting things. I keep demon thieves from stealing the artifacts in my shop, Ancient Magic. That means fighting demons."

"So what were you protecting back there?"

I grinned. "You, silly."

He laughed. "You'll have a hard time tomorrow if we don't get these healed."

"Yeah, I know. Can the clerk send up a healer?"

"At this hour? We'd have to go to the emergency room."

"Ugh." That sounded freaking awful.

"I could take care of it." His green gaze met mine. Tension thrummed across my skin, like the air vibrated with it.

"One of your halfbreed Mage gifts is healing?"

"Unfortunately, no." He smiled, and his fangs, which were normally retracted, lengthened a bit. Not enough to be gross, but enough to make fear race through me. "But vampire blood has healing abilities."

"Ew."

"Rude."

"Yeah, well that sounds risky. I don't want to turn into a vampire."

"You won't and you know it. We reproduce just like everyone else."

Did he *have* to talk about sex right now? When he was sitting so close to me and looking so damned good? I was kinda scared of him, especially when his fangs were out, but I was also kinda a moron when presented with a face as pretty as his.

Freaking embarrassing.

My arm hurt so bad I'd have sworn it had been amputated. "So you swear I won't turn into a vampire?"

"On my honor."

I wanted to make a quip about not being able to trust his honor, but something held my tongue. As much as he frightened me and pissed me off, I had a feeling that his honor was important to him.

More than that—he stuck by it.

He'd have to, considering that he was the element of vampire society that upheld the law.

"And will there be any side effects?" I asked.

"No."

A memory flashed in my mind—something I'd been wondering about.

"Hey." I stared at him until his gaze met mine, then had to force myself to hold it. "When we were running, you stayed behind me. But you're fast as lightning. Was that on purpose?"

"Coincidence."

Lie. It was so clear in his eyes. He'd stayed back there to protect me.

"Okay." I sucked in a deep breath. "Then just do it. It hurts like hell."

"Okay." He raised his wrist to his lips. His fangs lengthened another few millimeters, and he bit into his flesh.

I winced, but he seemed to kinda like it.

Okay, weird kinks ahead.

I watched, riveted, as he withdrew his fangs. Two puncture marks pearled with blood. He raised the wrist to the cut on my arm and smeared his blood over the wound.

Warmth flowed through me, followed quickly by a floaty pleasure that was entirely unfamiliar. Amazing.

I'd never done drugs, but I had a feeling that this was something like how that would feel. At least, I'd pay a lot of money for it, like any addict.

The flesh at my arm was smeared with my blood and his, but the wound was beginning to knit back together.

I glanced up at Ares, who was watching me intently. There was something unreadable in his dark eyes. Dark and hot and a little frightening. Whatever it was, it made my skin heat and my breath come quickly.

He broke the stare to inspect the wound at my arm. Apparently satisfied, he moved to the one at my waist. Having his hands so close to me sent a shiver racing over my skin.

I held my breath as he ran his wrist gently over the wound. It didn't even hurt. But maybe that was my distraction and excitement. My waist healed even more quickly than my arm. As soon as it was done, Ares surged to his feet.

"That should do it." He stalked away from me.

The moment was broken.

I sagged against the chair, grateful. I didn't have time to be attracted to the guy who held my life in his hands. And it was *stupid.*

"What about your chest?" I asked. "You had a cut."

He turned back and pulled aside the torn fabric of his shirt, revealing an expanse of muscular chest that was devoid of any wound. Blood covered the surface, but no cut.

"I'm full of vampire blood," he says. "I heal myself."

"Of course."

"You should be creating more blood cells pretty quickly now. You'll be at full strength in a few hours." He turned, as if he were uncomfortable all of a sudden, and picked up the phone.

He ordered room service, asking for anything that had a lot of cheese. And a steak, presumably for himself.

He hung up and turned to me. "I'm going to call some of my men here. They can scout out the station—see if there are any other entrances that are less guarded."

"Nice."

"Yeah. Save us some time while you heal up. Do you need

them to bring you anything? Change of clothes, that kind of thing?"

"No. I'll conjure what I need. When will they be here?"

"Ten minutes."

Good. That was just enough time. I stood. "I'm going to get a quick shower."

Really quick, because I didn't want to be naked when a bunch of vampires showed up in the suite.

There was only one vampire I wanted to be naked around, and I knew what a bad idea that was.

CHAPTER EIGHT

Because I had no shame, I chose the larger bedroom and bathroom for myself. It was a grand affair that entered onto the living room, and I shut that door as soon as I walked in.

I showered in eight minutes flat. After scrubbing myself dry and conjuring a new set of clothes—this T-shirt featured Bucky, the one-fanged comic strip cat—I went into the main room of the suite.

Ares hadn't yet showered, but then, he didn't have clean clothes.

"Better?" he asked.

"Much."

A knock sounded on the door. He opened it to reveal six vampires. They were all as tall as he was, and almost as muscular, but they lacked the same power. Whereas these guys looked like they could beat the shit out of a biker gang, Ares looked like he could tear the heads off the same biker gang without dropping his beer.

They filed into the room, their gazes trained on their boss. They had the look of soldiers, which they might as well have been.

I took a seat on the couch and watched.

The vampire on the far left stepped forward and handed Ares a duffle bag. "The things you requested, sir."

"Thank you, Owen." Ares took the bag and gave them their orders. They'd scout out the entire area around the clock tower, looking for an entrance that was guarded by less than two dozen demons.

They nodded, their gazes firm, then turned to file out of the room.

"You run a tight ship," I said.

"It's best that way."

Another knock sounded on the door.

My stomach grumbled as if it knew room service was here. When Ares opened the door to reveal a young clerk with a name tag reading "Bryan" and a white cart full of covered plates, my stomach grumbled again.

Bryan wheeled the cart into the room and set up the food at the table in front of the window. My foot bounced as I waited, and my stomach ached. I was ready to pounce on it like a tiger on a gazelle. Or a rat on a block of cheese, more appropriately.

Ares tipped him and he left.

"Help yourself," he said. "I'm going to shower."

He went to the other bedroom, and I tucked in, uncovering plate after plate of cheesy pasta, cheese sandwiches, four-cheese pizza, baked brie, and a cheeseburger. There was a giant steak that I left for him. If it'd been stuffed with gorgonzola, I'd have considered it. As it was...nope.

"Thank you, Ares," I murmured.

I dug in, famished after the fight from earlier. By the time Ares made it out of the shower, I'd polished off most of the cheesy entrees.

He eyed my empty plates. "Nicely done."

I leaned back, satisfied. "What can I say? I'm a pro."

"That you are." He sat across from me and uncovered the

steak, then cut in. He'd changed into new clothes, but they were identical to the last ones. Dark jeans and a black shirt. I'd bet twenty bucks there was a leather jacket back in his room.

He looked damned good in his uniform, though. It suited him. And were his eyes a bit brighter? His hair shinier?

"You look different," I said.

"I changed clothes."

"No, I mean, your hair and eyes and all that. And you look a bit bigger, too." It was freaky.

His gaze met mine, unreadable. "My men brought me some blood. It perks me up." He grinned, his fangs showing. "The bottled stuff tastes like shit, but it gets the job done."

"Oh." Well, I guessed I was glad it wasn't me. "Hey, what was with your weird sword made of shadow? You didn't conjure that, right?"

"No. My father gave me that blade. It's enchanted to appear at will."

"Wow. Neat trick."

"I don't always use it. Sometimes I prefer hand-to-hand. But you clearly have more magic than you use."

I jumped. "That was out of the blue."

"Not really. We just fought off a dozen demons, and you insisted on using only a sword. Magic would have helped you."

"You didn't use magic."

"My speed and strength are basically magic." The grin he gave me was cocky, but well deserved. "And the shadow blade is more than enough."

"Yeah, yeah." I sipped the wine that Bryan had brought, wishing it was Four Roses.

"Back to your magic. Why didn't you use it? I can sense it on you. You *have* it. There's more to you than just a Conjurer."

"I'm a Seeker too."

"That's not what I'm talking about. You're special and you

know it. But I want to know how special and why you don't use that to save your own life."

Maybe I can't use it! I wanted to scream. First, I was incapable. I'd never used my FireSoul powers to steal a gift. And second, using it would get me killed if anyone discovered I was a FireSoul. There was a cell in the Prison for Magical Miscreants with *FireSoul* written right on the door. Cass had stayed there a while, and it'd been bad.

I wasn't going to end up there myself.

"You're delusional," I said. "But you look good in your uniform."

His brows rose, surprised. Then they lowered. "You're trying to distract me."

I grinned. "Did it work? You're very handsome."

"I'm not falling for it." His lips twitched. "Though it is true that I am very handsome, it's also true that you have magic that you're hiding. And I want to know why."

I stretched my arms over my head, yawning. "Wow, it's late. I've suffered a lot of blood loss, and you're so wrong that it's boring me." I stood. "Bedtime. But we're getting started early, right?"

From the look in his eyes, I hadn't fooled him. But maybe I'd gotten a reprieve. "Yes. Be ready at six a.m., and we'll get a report from my men. We'll go from there."

"Aye aye." I hurried to my room and shut the door, then leaned against the wall.

He was getting nosy. And he was too powerful and well-connected to be easy to ignore.

I reached up and touched the collar at my neck. I was down to two days.

A shiver raced over me.

Ares's suspicion of me might not be an issue if I couldn't convince the Vampire Court that I was innocent and to take this thing off. Unless I only had to convince Ares?

That'd be ideal.

The light under the door blinked out, turning dark. He'd finished his steak. And had gone into his bedroom, it seemed.

The memory of a slice of cake under one of the domed silver platters flashed in my mind's eye. I hadn't had a chance to eat it because I'd wanted to get out from under his scrutiny.

But now…

I crept out into the living room. His door was shut, but light shined from the crack underneath.

The cake was still covered in the middle of the table. I was about to pick it up when a noise sounded in his room.

My ears perked up.

Voices?

I crept over to his door, careful to stand near the wall so he couldn't see a shadow of my feet in the crack beneath the door. I breathed as silently as I could, straining my ears.

"What do you mean, evidence has been presented against her?" he said.

Her? Did that mean me?

"An eyewitness has come forward," a woman's voice said.

How was she in there? Magic, if I had to bet.

"When?" Ares demanded.

"Just an hour ago. He came from the Shadowlands. Said that he saw her kill Marin." Her voice was very formal.

"We're weighing his testimony strongly," said another feminine voice. This one was just as formal. "But it doesn't look good for Phoenix Knight."

I swallowed hard, sweat breaking out over my skin.

Someone was framing me.

And these two women were important. Were they the other sides of the Vampire Court?

It made sense. They would be the only people to talk to Ares as an equal rather than their master.

Shit shit shit.

"I don't believe that she killed Marin." Ares's voice was cold. "I'm convinced the murderer is still out there."

"Why would you believe her?" the first woman asked.

"Because it's my job to find the truth. As you well know, Magisteria."

"You had better be correct. Marin was important."

"I agree. You *know* how much I agree. But this is deeper than Marin. And I will be right. My loyalty to the Vampire Court is unbreakable. We are the foundation upon which our society rests. I would not risk that."

The heaviness of Ares's voice made me shiver. He had a lot on his shoulders, and he respected that.

My life included.

At least he was committed to helping me prove my innocence.

"You have two days." Magisteria's voice was so cold that it was obvious she didn't believe him. "Then her time is up. Non-negotiable."

Shit. It was suddenly hard to breathe. And cold.

"It will be done." Ares's voice was so confident that it should have made me feel better.

But right now, nothing was going to make me feel better. There was someone actively working to frame me. And the other two members of the Vampire Court were *definitely* not on my side.

Shaking, I crept back across the living room and into my room, where I fell into bed.

I was screwed.

It was one of those dreams that felt real because it had once *been* real. Even though I knew I wasn't really trapped in the Monster's dungeon anymore, my mind was there while I slept.

The cold dark was too familiar to mistake. The damp stone

floor beneath my butt was etched into my memory, as was the sound of the dripping water in the corner and the scuttling of rats.

"Cass? Del?" I whispered.

In the dark, no one responded.

A sob rose in my throat, but I bit it down, afraid for the guard to hear.

I was alone.

Which meant this was the time before they'd been captured. I'd been the first child taken by the Monster, when I was only fourteen. The six months I'd spent alone in his dark dungeon cell had been the worst of my life.

I would never experience anything that terrible ever again.

Except in my dreams.

I tried with everything I could to escape the nightmare, but I was trapped.

Here, I was always trapped.

Footsteps sounded outside the door. I pressed myself back into the corner, trying to become invisible. If I could sink into the stone I would. I'd become part of this terrible dungeon if it meant I could escape whatever was outside in the hall.

When the door creaked open and light flooded into the dark cell, my eyes went blind. It'd been days since I'd seen light.

"Time to go." The gruff voice belonged to the mean guard. The one who held my arm too tightly and hissed threats in my ears. He liked doing that. I could sense it, and it creeped me out.

I surged to my feet despite the fear that wanted to keep me pressed against the wall. I'd learned the hard way that resistance didn't work. It just made him meaner. And I was a skinny four-teen—not able to fight and still unable to conjure a weapon. Though my mother was an excellent Conjurer, my skills were slow to develop.

How I wished they'd been faster, that I could conjure a sword and plunge it into the gut of the horrible man who would drag me to an even more horrible fate.

On leaden feet, I approached him, my limbs rebelling but my mind forcing them to work.

My will was stronger than my fear. It always had been.

"Come on, now," the guard barked. He gripped my arm in a fist, squeezing hard enough to leave bruises.

He dragged me down the hall, walking almost too fast to keep up with. When he threw me into another, larger cell, my heart dropped.

No. I shuddered. Not this again.

Sometimes they took me out to bathe. That would not happen today.

A man lay strapped to a table in the middle of the room. He was about my parents' age, with mousy brown hair and magic that smelled like a forest fire.

Behind him, the Monster stood. He wore a fancy suit and had the face of a banker—totally nondescript and boring.

Terrifying.

I knew what he was capable of. And that made him terrifying.

"Are you ready to use your gift?" The Monster's voice was so precise and sharp that it could slice lengthwise through a hair.

"I don't have a gift," I squeaked. Sweat began to drip down my back.

"Lies. You are a FireSoul. You will embrace your gift."

My eyes darted to the man, who'd begun to struggle. He knew what I'd have to do in order to *embrace my gift.*

Kill him and steal his magic.

I shook my head and backed up.

I would not kill that man. I *could* not.

"You'll do it, or we'll kill your mother," the Monster said.

There was so much honest promise in his voice that a sob tore through my chest. I hadn't seen my mother since they'd stolen me from my family months ago. They'd taken her and my father as well.

Last time the Monster had brought me to this room, he'd threatened to kill my father if I didn't do as he said. That time, I'd been unable to kill the man on the table. I'd vomited and passed out.

When I'd woken, the Monster had shown me a vision of my father being run through with a sword.

Because of me.

I trembled where I stood, the Monster's gaze burning into me. It flayed my skin from my bones.

I had only my mother left, according to him. I hadn't seen her, but now I'd have to save her by killing this man? He struggled on the table, trying to break free.

Horror opened a deep chasm inside my chest.

The Monster would live up to his promise—I knew that from experience.

"You'll do it. *Now.*"

I jumped, shaking. The memory of my mother flashed in my mind. I couldn't watch her be stabbed with a sword. I couldn't. She was my mother.

And this man—he might be a bad man. My mother wasn't bad.

"Do it!" The Monster's bland eyes blazed with conviction.

He wanted to train me to work for him. It was my best guess. And he would succeed. Because I couldn't lose my mother.

Shaking, I approached the table.

"No! Don't do this," the man begged.

How had I gotten here, ready to commit murder? I was only fourteen. I wasn't a murderer.

But I would be. For my mother.

I reached up, curling my hands around his throat. I knew the mechanics of this magic. My mother had explained it. I had to kill him, then ignite the fire in my soul that would steal his magic.

But she'd also said *never* to use it. That it was evil to kill and steal another's magic.

I sobbed, pulling my hands back.

"Do it!" the Monster commanded. "Or your mother dies."

I sucked in a ragged breath and clasped my hands around the man's neck. He thrashed, but he was bound so tightly it did him no good.

Tears poured down my face as I squeezed. Nausea rose in me, and my mother's voice echoed in my head, telling me not to do this. It was evil. It would reveal me to the world and get me killed.

It was evil.

No, no, no.

I couldn't kill this man.

The nausea rose, overwhelming me.

I heaved away from the man, falling to my knees and retching up bile.

"No!" the Monster roared. "Weak!"

I vomited out my hopes and fears and rage and weakness as the Monster shrieked behind me. My tears blinded me as my head spun.

Finally, I keeled over, passing out on the cold stone floor.

CHAPTER NINE

I woke with a gasp. Tears wet my face.

Shit.

I stumbled out of bed, desperate to get away from...from everything. I hadn't dreamed of my time in the Monster's dungeon in years. And I'd never had a dream that vivid.

When Cass, Del, and I had escaped from him, we'd used magic that had blasted away our memories. Both of them had remembered much of their pasts already, but not me.

It looked like I was finally starting to remember.

And what I was finding...

It was terrible. Tears burned my eyes as I made my way to the shower.

Had I been responsible for my mother and father's deaths? Because I couldn't follow the Monster's orders?

No wonder I had such an aversion to stealing powers, even in instances where my prey would be someone so totally evil that he deserved to die.

Not that the man in my dream had deserved to die. He hadn't. His face still haunted me. Like Marin's.

Shakily, I turned on the shower and washed away the tears. I almost wanted to wash away the memories, but they were all I had of my parents.

Until now, I'd remembered *nothing*.

I couldn't lose them. Because apparently they'd loved me. Tried to protect me from the Monster when he'd stolen me.

And as a result, he'd killed them.

Killed them because I couldn't follow his orders.

I stumbled in the shower, almost going to my knees. The pain that tore through my chest was greater than any I'd ever felt.

The wound from today? Nothing.

Water slid around the golden collar at my throat, reminding me of all that was coming at me if I didn't get my shit together.

So I dragged in a breath and got my shit together. Slowly, but surely, I managed it.

If that time in the Monster's dungeon had taught me anything, it was how to get my shit together.

I scrubbed up quickly, then hopped out and dried off. The clothes from last night would do the trick, so I put them on and headed out into the living room.

Ares was already there, eating a breakfast that room service had delivered. Memories from last night collided in my mind. Him, healing me. Him, defending me to his fellow members of the Vampire Court.

Them, saying my time was almost up.

"Sleep all right?" he asked.

"Yeah. Totally." I nodded in a way that I hoped seemed genuine but probably came off as a bit crazy.

I joined him and poured myself a cup of coffee, then dug into the pancakes. "What did your minions say?"

He arched a brow, and I hated myself for thinking it was kinda sexy. Honestly, it was supercilious and annoying.

Almost.

"My men said that there isn't another entrance to the clock tower that's unguarded. But there might be an entrance in the train station. They observed people coming and going from a section of the station that appears to be blocked off."

"Okay, that's kinda promising. When do we check it out? During rush hour? The trains will be busiest around seven."

"That's what I was thinking. See if we can get some cover from commuters. If these people have been operating in secret underneath the noses of normal supernaturals, they'll want to lie low. They probably won't have a horde of demons roaming around the station."

"I like it." I checked the clock on the desk. "That gives us forty-five minutes."

"Enough time to eat and make our way over there."

"Perfect." I dug into the pancakes, planning to polish them off and then move on to the cheese omelet that he'd ordered for me. I had a feeling that I was going to need the energy for today.

~

The morning was brisk and chilly as we crossed the street toward Saint Pancras station. We passed the big brick building and the bell tower on top, and headed for the station behind.

As soon as we entered, we were caught up in the rush of people going to work or on holiday. We followed them into the main part of the station, an enormous rectangular space with a tall glass ceiling and shops on either side. The building had been built in the nineteenth century, and looked it.

I liked historic places, but this one had me a bit nervous. Probably because I was here to find a way to get this death collar off my neck.

My gaze darted, searching for demon guards. There were none that I could see, but that didn't put me at ease.

We stuck close to the shops along the side of the building, blending with the crowd as we crept toward the area that was closest to the bell tower. The shops were less busy back here, so we pretended to be window-shopping.

Subtly, I called upon my dragon sense, feeding it my desire to find an entrance to the bell tower. After a while, it caught hold, pulling me toward the back right of the station.

"This way." I took Ares's hand, as if we were just a couple out having a stroll.

I pulled him toward a darkened area of the station. There was a corridor leading off to the right. The sign indicating that the restrooms were down that way had been modified with an *Out of Order* note. Three orange cones blocked the way.

"This is what your men were talking about." I walked straight for it.

"Agreed."

As soon as we neared the cones, I was hit with the strongest sense that I shouldn't go back there. It was under construction, and the maintenance staff were probably hard at work fixing the toilets. I couldn't possibly bother them.

"Feel that?" I murmured.

"Same as last night. Stronger though."

"Good thing we had practice, then." Whoever was in this building, they really liked their repelling charms. And considering we were in Britain where everyone liked to queue up and follow the signs politely, this was a good charm. It probably repelled 99.99% of everyone who wandered back here.

Except us.

I hurried through the cones and into the darkened corridor. It was about fifteen feet wide and twenty-five feet deep.

Slowly, I crept deeper, Ares at my side.

True to the sign, it smelled of broken toilets. The bathroom door was cracked slightly open, but my dragon sense had no interest in that. The wall at the end of the hall was built of brick that hadn't been scrubbed clean in a long while.

My dragon sense tugged hard toward it. "I think we need to go through that wall."

Ares nodded and we started toward it.

Almost immediately, it became difficult to walk. As if we were walking through transparent pudding. It felt like I had hundred-pound weights attached to my ankles.

"This is weird." Even my voice came out slowly.

Ares could move quicker than me, maybe because he was stronger, but I had no idea. He was a few feet in front of me when it became even harder to walk. I was still at least ten feet from the back wall, and it felt like I was dragging myself through wet cement.

Someone *definitely* didn't want folks to reach that wall. Unease shivered through me, making the hair on the back of my neck stand upright.

We were so slow this way, and vulnerable. My heart thudded. Demons could come upon us at any moment, and we'd have a damned hard time defending ourselves like this.

I felt like a sitting duck.

"We have a problem," I muttered, my speech slow.

Ares glanced back. He was a half-dozen feet ahead. He stepped back and reached out for me. I strained to take his hand, gasping when his magic flowered through me.

Suddenly, it was easier to walk. The cement turned back to pudding and finally to water. It was still difficult, but I could at least do it.

Together, we used Ares's strange magic to walk through the enchantment. When we stopped in front of the wall, I reached out, trying to push my hand through it.

No luck.

"It's real." I gazed at the wall, searching for any clue at all. You could just never tell—normally it was a small thing that would give it away.

A few feet over, about waist height, there was a small circular area in the brick that looked slightly worn down and shiny. As if something had repeatedly rubbed against it.

That was weird.

It was roughly the size of the Medallion that we'd taken from PTA lady.

I held out my hand to Ares. "Give me the medallion."

He dug it out of his pocket and handed it over. Still holding his hand, I shuffled over to the spot in the wall. I held my breath as I pressed the medallion to the door.

Nothing happened.

I flipped the medallion over and tried it that way.

Magic streaked through the medallion, warming underneath my palm. It shivered up my arm and through my chest.

"Bingo." The words had barely left my mouth when the bricks shimmered and disappeared, revealing a door.

I grinned at Ares, then pressed it open and stepped inside the dimly lit room. It was large and ornately done, with carved dark wood and gold accents.

Two guards stood behind a wide wooden desk. Not demons this time, but Mages. From the scent of their magic, they were a Fire Mage and an Ice Mage.

Their bored eyes met mine and widened with interest, as if they had expected to recognize me but hadn't. But they didn't attack.

I glanced at Ares, silently asking how we should play this. Apparently that medallion was a key to get in, and the guards didn't yet recognize that we shouldn't be here.

"Medallion, please," said the dark- haired guard. His voice was uninterested, but it could be an act. His eyes were sharp.

Might as well try to bluff our way through this.

I handed over the medallion, trying not to be too obvious about holding my breath.

He took the medallion and studied it, then looked at a large book on the desk and flipped through it.

His sharp gaze darted up to meet mine. "You're not Maria Forebear. She's been dead for ten years."

"Nope. Not Maria," I said as I glanced at Ares.

He nodded briefly, which I took to mean *time to fight.*

"How'd you get this?" the guard demanded.

Since I was certain he wouldn't like my answer, I conjured a bat instead. I swung at his head, just hard enough that it should knock him out, while Ares reached for the guard nearest him.

My guy was so fast that he managed to blast off a small fireball before my bat collided. I dodged it by a hair. The heat seared my cheek as it flew by. A millisecond later, my bat collided with his head. *Crack!* He collapsed onto the desk in front of him.

Ares dragged his guy over the desk and punched him so hard I swore I saw stars form over his head. He slumped, out cold.

"Not bad," I said.

"Not bad yourself." He dragged his guy behind the desk. "Now let's get these guys tied up."

"On it." I stowed the bat under the desk and conjured two pairs of metal handcuffs. Rope would have worked if one of these guys wasn't a Fire Mage, but I didn't want them burning their restraints off.

We made quick work of binding their wrists and feet, then shoved them under the desk.

Ares leaned over the open book that the guard had consulted. I did the same, and an image of PTA lady frowned out of her official portrait.

"Looks like PTA lady is pretending to be dead," I said.

"Wonder why?"

"Maybe you don't want these guys knowing you're alive."

"Or she betrayed them."

I thought back to her icy eyes. "Yeah, very possibly. But let's get out of here."

"There could be leads in their book."

"I don't think so. My seeker sense isn't pointing that way." In face, my dragon sense was tugging me toward the hallway behind the desk. It was as dark and ornate as the room out front, with carved mahogany scrollwork at the ceiling and dim golden lighting.

Whoever these folks were, they sure took themselves seriously.

"You sure?" Ares asked.

"I'm betting my life on it, aren't I?" With this collar around my neck, every decision I made had to be correct.

"True." He gestured. "Lead on."

We moved silently down the hall and fortunately saw no one. This felt more like a place of work than a residence, and apparently no one had clocked in yet.

At the end of the hall, two wide wooden doors loomed. They were like beacons, calling to me.

"Definitely through there," I said.

Ares pushed one of the heavy doors open, and I slipped inside. The air was suddenly cooler. Different.

I leaned my head back to look above me and swayed. "Whoa."

We were at the bottom of a square tower—the bell tower. Overhead, a tall stone staircase wrapped around the walls. The entire inner area was open, so you could fall right off the edge of the stairs and plummet to your death.

It was the intimidating pomp and circumstance version of a stairway.

"These people take themselves very seriously," Ares said.

"Exactly what I was thinking." I stepped onto the first stair. "Might as well head up."

The stairs were wide, about seven feet across, and made of gray marble. They were slick as I climbed, Ares at my back.

We were about a third of the way to the top when magic shivered through the air.

"Incoming," I said.

The stairs began to move. Of-freaking-course. I just couldn't get away from this handy trick. But instead of becoming a simple split staircase like before, we entered an MC Escher Wonderland. Staircases popped out of nowhere, going all directions. Up, down, sideways, twisted.

There were at least two dozen options for getting to the top, and I'd bet big money that one wrong step would equal a quick drop.

"Which way?" Ares asked. "You're good at this kind of thing."

That I was. I called on my dragon sense, feeding it my desire to get to the top in one piece.

To my annoyance, it tugged me to the set of stairs that was sideways. As in, I'd have to walk with my body parallel to the floor and pray that magic kept my feet glued to the stairs and my body in the air.

I pointed to it.

"You've got to be joking," Ares said.

"Nope. Of course it's the most dangerous-looking one. This is a challenge, remember?" I pointed up. "And whatever is up there is apparently worth protecting."

"Fine, but I'll go first."

"I don't need a hero," I said, but immediately regretted it. If he wanted to risk his life, let him. And he could probably transport himself before he hit the ground. Not to mention the healing powers.

He gave me a wry look and passed me, then stepped on the sideways stairs. He sucked in a deep breath, then twisted his body so that he was parallel to the ground below.

He stuck. It was a weird sight, but he didn't fall.

Slowly, he made his way up the stairs. I hurried after him, needing speed to add to my courage. And I needed to keep going in order to tell him which way to go next.

My stomach lurched as I climbed the stairs. The other staircases loomed out of the corners of my vision, but I ignored them, trying to keep my gaze on Ares's back ahead of me.

There were three options ahead of Ares. Up, left, and upside down. The upside-down staircase actually went upward, but it had a smooth top and stairs on its underside.

"You're not going to like this," I said. "But you're going to have to take the stairs that are upside down."

"Of course." His voice was so dry it could have been kindling. But he didn't hesitate, just stepped onto the upside-down staircase and started walking. "This is weird."

"Way weird," I said after I'd joined him. Gravity was going the wrong way, but I still felt like I was hanging upside down.

My heart was pounding in my ears by the time we made it onto a normal staircase. My dragon sense led us through a few more crazy options—including a sideways spiral—but we eventually made it to the landing at the top. It was wide, with doors behind us and no railing in front. The stairs returned to normal as soon as we'd stepped on the platform.

I pressed my back against the wall, panting.

Ares joined me. "You're no ordinary Seeker."

Shit. And he was right. Seekers could find *things*. Lost car keys, a red shirt in the mall, even treasure in some circumstances. But what I'd just done? I'd asked my dragon sense to find my *desire*. My desire for a safe way out. I was almost as sure as Ares that a Seeker couldn't do what I'd just done.

"My mom was a very powerful Seeker," I bluffed. "She passed it on to me."

"Not true." His gaze met mine, serious and thoughtful. "You're not a very good liar."

Actually, I was a *great* liar. I'd been living lies my whole life, keeping my FireSoul a secret.

But Ares was really good at sniffing out the untruths, it seemed.

"We need to get a move on." I turned to the door behind me, hoping that there wouldn't be anyone on the other side.

I got lucky. The large space felt empty—probably because the stairs themselves were supposed to act as the guards.

They hadn't counted on a FireSoul showing up.

"What is this place?" Ares asked.

"It looks like the card catalogue at the library." We were inside the clock tower—which was pretty awesome, frankly, with the gears on one wall controlling the clocks hands. The ceiling was the underside of the peaked roof.

And down here on the floor were tall, dark wooden cabinets with tiny drawers. Hundreds of them. Just like the library.

I moved toward one and pulled open a drawer. Tiny gold index cards were filed neatly, but according to no system that I could determine. I pulled one out.

"It says that the previous leader of the Order of the Magica had betrayed all his business partners to achieve his position."

"I'd heard rumors of that," Ares said. "It's why he was removed from office."

"Huh. Okay." I put the card back and pulled open another drawer. "This card says that the last winner of the Little Miss Magic beauty pageant was actually an enchanted orangutan."

"I can't speak to the truth of that one, unfortunately."

"Child beauty pageants not your thing?"

"No. I prefer cat fashion shows on the animal channel."

The delivery was so genuine that I laughed. "Really?"

"No. Do those actually exist?"

"On the internet, definitely." I put the card back and withdrew another. "Moira Deitreich, that famous fae actress from the forties, was apparently an Allied spy during the war. She used her enchantment ability to help them win."

Ares read from a card. "There was once a hidden race of dwarves that mined so much gold they went mad. They were so obsessed with keeping it secret from the world that they drove themselves insane."

I stepped back and glanced around this place. "So, this place is full of information?"

"Information that people shouldn't know."

"Secrets. Just like Laphraig said. The charm was shrouded in secrets."

"Literally and figuratively."

"How do we use this to find Marin's killer?" I asked. "If he was killed for something that he knew—like a secret—how the hell do we find it amongst all these?"

"If it's even here," Ares said. "It could be—"

The door slammed open from behind us. I spun. Before I'd completed the motion, a blue potion bomb had exploded against my shoulder, drenching me in a glittery blue liquid.

My head spun, and my eyes rolled back in my head. I slammed into the ground. The world went black.

CHAPTER TEN

Pain seared my skull as I woke. My eyelids were scratchy, and my mouth felt like I was trying to chew on a sheep's fluffy butt.

Blech.

I tried to spit out the cottony feeling, but it did no good. My eyes burned as I opened them and took stock of my surroundings.

I was in a dungeon made of stone.

My heart jumped into my throat, and sweat broke out on my skin. I heaved upward, panic a living beast inside my chest. It clawed at me, ready to tear into my organs and feast.

Panting, I searched for Cass and Del.

But instead of my *deirfiúr*, there was a large masculine body sprawled out on the ground next to me. I blinked.

Shit. That was Ares.

And I was an adult. I wasn't a kid trapped in the Monster's dungeon any longer.

Thank fates.

I sagged back against the wall, the sweat chilling on my skin. Panting, I tried to get ahold of myself.

First, where the hell were we?

We'd been hit by potion bombs containing a sleeping spell and were now in some creepy kind of dungeon. The room was a small rectangle with an arched stone ceiling. Three walls were made of stone, but the one across from me was made of wood.

That was weird.

This place must be old.

I nudged Ares with my boot, still so exhausted from the potion that it was difficult to move. "Ares, wake up."

He groaned, then leapt to his feet so fast that I almost shrieked. He was in full vampire mode now. Gleaming white fangs extended, and black claws protruded from his fingertips. His stance was *I'm ready to tear your head off.*

"Chill, dude, it's just me."

His gaze cleared almost immediately. He straightened. "Sorry. Instinct."

"Not caught by surprise too often?"

"No." He turned, inspecting the room. "This is quaint."

I laughed, then dragged myself to my feet. "How long have we been out?"

How much time had been taken off my 72 hours?

Ares glanced at his watch. "Only thirty minutes."

Whew. "Can you transport us out of here?"

"I can try." He walked toward me and took my hand. His magic swelled, bringing with it the scent of a cold winter morning and a warm caress against my skin.

But we didn't go anywhere.

"Warded against transporting, as all proper dungeons are," he said.

"It's fine." I dropped his hand. "We'll find a way out."

There was a big door set into the wooden wall, but no lock that we could pick. Just a flat expanse of wood.

We both walked to the wall—the only possible weakness in the room—and reached out to touch it.

Electricity surged through me, slamming me into the stone

wall at my back. Ares followed, hit by the same bolt of magic that had singed my hair.

My head spun and I blinked, trying to clear my vision. "Oh, shit."

Ares winced and straightened. "That way isn't an option."

"You can't get through that enchantment like you did the weird thick air back in the station?" It'd been so strange how he'd been able to cut through it.

"About that." His gaze met mine. "That strange, thick air wasn't an enchantment. It was the entrance to another realm."

Another *realm*? "You didn't think to mention this?"

"Between the guards and the Escher staircase, we didn't exactly have a lot of time."

"Fair enough. Then explain."

"The interior of this building is in another realm. A bit like the Shadowlands. It's on Earth, but not quite. I have the ability to walk to other realms, which was why I could get through that weird air."

"Are all vampires able to do that?"

"All of them can travel between our realm and Earth, but not necessarily other realms."

"Guess I'm lucky I'm with you, then."

A creaking noise sounded from the wooden wall. My attention snapped to it.

A little window had opened, and an ugly face peered inside. Whether it was man or demon, I couldn't tell.

"Awake, are you?" His voice was rough as steel wool.

"Yeah. Thanks for the hospitality," I said.

"Well, you'll be enjoying it for a while. Until the Head Sector decides to see you." He grinned showing off his jagged yellow teeth. "It may be a while."

The little door slammed shut.

I looked at Ares. "That doesn't sound promising."

"No." He inspected the room. "We need to find a way out."

"Agreed." Since the wooden wall was entirely out of the question, I studied the rest of the room. The arched stone ceiling looked ancient, and there were centuries worth of graffiti carved into the walls. "This place is ancient."

"We're one story underground, I think."

I studied the graffiti carved into the back wall. There was so much jumbled on there that it was hard to determine what any of it said.

"Anything good written on there?" Ares asked.

"Maybe." I approached and peered hard at some scribbles. "Might as well look."

He joined me. I shifted toward the other side of the room. As much as I didn't want to use my dragon sense again—he was going to definitely figure out something was up—we really needed it right now. If there was a way out of here, I wanted to find it.

The best way to find anything was obvious for a FireSoul.

As carefully as I could, I called on my magic, trying to keep my signature repressed. If I was careful, he wouldn't even be able to sense that I was doing anything at all.

Please help me find a way out.

I envisioned an escape tunnel in the wall or learning a way to blast the door down, hoping that it would help jumpstart my dragon sense.

I'd gotten the briefest clue and was walking toward it when Ares turned to me. "You're using your magic. Why?"

I killed the connection with my magic. "No idea what you're talking about."

I studied the graffiti etched high above my head, even though I desperately wanted to look at what was scratched on the lower part of the wall. But I couldn't go right to it or it would look obvious.

"You're doing a terrible job of pretending to be normal, Nix."

I grinned back at him. "I never said I was normal."

"You know what I mean. With your magic."

I sighed and turned back to the wall. "No comment. Let's look for a way out."

"Fine."

I studied the graffiti. There were the usual names and dates, along with poems and drawings. Some folks had spent a long time here.

But had it always been a dungeon?

Nah. The construction was too weird for a dungeon. Who would build a dungeon with only three stone walls? It had probably been modified later to house unwilling occupants.

I crouched low to inspect the writing that had called to me.

What the heck?

It was in Latin. That was freaking weird.

Because of our line of work, Del, Cass, and I were all interested in history. But I'd never been terribly fond of the Romans. I didn't like conquerors and colonialists. As a result, I only knew a bit of Latin. Not enough to translate all of this.

"Can you read Latin?" I asked.

"Some." He approached. "A lot of our older documents are in Latin."

I pointed to the four lines of engraved text. "Give this a whirl."

He crouched next to me and studied the text, then began to read, "Place any of the wine amphora on the five points of the star. Use the elder wood stylus to trace the etchings on the floor. Light the wine on fire. Escape."

"What the hell does that mean?" I asked.

"No idea."

"Say it again. Exactly how it is written."

He repeated it. I leaned against the wall, studying the room and mulling it over. "If it says place *any* of the wine amphora on the floor, that means there were a lot here."

"What were amphora?"

"Weirdly shaped clay jugs used by the Romans." I stared at the ceiling, and it hit me. "This used to be a storage facility for a Roman wine merchant."

"How the hell did you get that?"

I smirked at him. "Elementary, my dear Watson."

"You're still going to have to explain."

"The Romans often used underground storage vaults like this one. There's the Horreum in Narbonne, France and the tunnels in Exeter in the UK. One of their most desired trade goods when they conquered this part of the UK was wine. From the sound of that graffiti, this was where a wine merchant stored his stash."

"That seems like a stretch."

I shrugged. "It's archaeology. Lotta educated guesswork." I frowned, rethinking the inscription. "I think those are quick getaway instructions. This would have been the back of the merchant's property. Most of his stuff is underground, so there are no doors or windows. Say he had to run for it... He'd want an out. Like an escape tunnel."

"So he wrote the instructions on the wall?"

"Why not? If he passed the place down to his kids, they'd want to know how to operate the escape hatch."

"And in all the times this has been a dungeon, no one has used it?"

"Wasn't easy to find, was it?" I asked. "You'd have to inspect all the graffiti, know Latin, and have enough of an understanding of Roman architecture and history to put it together. I couldn't have done it without your knowledge of Latin, and you couldn't have done it without my history smarts."

"All right. I'll buy it." He gave me an appraising look. "Are you planning to conjure some amphora and an elder wood stylus?"

"If we can find that star on the floor, then heck yeah." My heart sped. This was getting exciting. Normally I worked behind the desk and left the archaeological puzzle solving to Cass and Del.

Now it was my turn.

Though the stakes were higher than I was expecting.

I stood. "Let's find that star."

We circled the ground, studying it for any evidence of a star etched into the stones. The rock was so pockmarked and scratched that it was hard to make out any kind of pattern.

It took at least ten minutes, but finally, after I'd pretended it was one of those Magic Eye patterns from the '80s, I was able to make out a pattern.

"There." I pointed. "It's about ten feet across and in the back corner."

Ares crouched low, tilting his head. "Yeah, I see it. There's five points."

"Yep." I called upon my magic, envisioning five amphora containing wine. One by one, the slender clay jugs appeared on the ground. Their bottoms were pointed, so they leaned on their sides. Using a bit more of my power, I conjured a willow wood stylus. It was basically just a smoothed-out stick. A bit like a wand, really.

"Put them at the points of the star," I said.

Ares and I gently laid the amphora at the points of the star.

He stepped back. "Do you know how to light the wine on fire if it's inside the amphora? And is wine even flammable?"

"Nope and nope." I stepped into the middle of the star. "But it's all we've got, so I'm going to try. I just hope that something will happen to point me in the right direction."

"Works for me."

I knelt and reached out with the stylus, tracing the lines between the jugs. Magic shivered in the air as I worked, igniting a long-dead spell. My breath caught as I waited for the enchantment to take hold.

Come on, come on.

As soon as I'd traced the last line, the amphora exploded, sending shards of terra-cotta flying into the air.

"Whoa!" I stumbled back onto my butt. Pain pinched at my

neck. I rubbed it, my fingers coming away bloody. I'd been sliced by a terra-cotta shard. I prodded the wound. It was shallow. Whew.

Ares had a similar slice on his cheek.

"Are you all right?" he asked.

"Just a flesh wound."

His mouth kicked up at the corner. "Monty Python?"

"Of course." I studied the star. The broken terra-cotta was scattered on the ground, its inscribed lines filled with dark red wine. "I guess that's how I light it on fire."

"If it lights."

"Hopefully the magic in the star will help." I conjured a packet of matches, then struck one and tossed it into the wine.

Flames burst into the air, racing along the lines of the star until I was surrounded by them. A second later, the floor dropped out from under me.

My scream echoed as I fell into the darkness.

I slammed into the ground below. The air whooshed out of me.

I shouldn't have stood in the middle of the star.

"Nix!" Ares called down.

"Yeah, I'm here!" I looked up, my eyes tearing from the pain of landing on a stone. The dungeon was about ten feet above me.

Ares appeared at the edge of the hole. "Do you need me to get you out or should I join you?"

I turned in a circle, inspecting my circumstances. There was a passage leading away from the dungeon. It smelled of stale air and was dark and mysterious in a freaky way, but it was better than a locked cell.

"Come on in!" I called. "The water's great."

He jumped in, landing gracefully next to me. "Nicely done."

"Thanks. Let's see where this leads."

We entered the passage side by side. I limped a bit, but shook it off with every step. It was just large enough to fit us both. I was about to conjure a torch when Ares held out a hand. White light glowed from his palm, illuminating the passage.

"That's a very handy skill," I said.

He chuckled. "That was a bad pun."

"At least you laughed."

"My mistake." But I could hear the grin in his voice.

I smiled, too, then kicked myself. I didn't want to humanize him. Or like him. Both were dumb moves I couldn't afford.

We hurried though the corridor, which was paved with stone and so dusty and stale it clearly hadn't been used in millennia. Not since the Roman wine merchant had built the place, I'd bet.

"Wonder where this leads?" I murmured.

"Hopefully within the building. We need to find the Master of Secrets."

"I agree. We'll go to him of our own will. It'll look better than if we're dragged there as prisoners. Then we question him."

Ares nodded. The path began to slope upward slightly. Twenty yards later, it ended at a wooden wall.

"That looks newer than the passage," Ares said.

"Yeah." I knocked on it, grinning when it echoed hollowly. "There's a room beyond here."

"Move back."

I did.

Ares stepped up to the wall and kicked hard. The wood burst inward, splintering into fragments. There was a hole big enough to climb through.

He slipped through first—which seemed to be a habit of his—and I followed.

The room on the other side was full of old crap. There was no better word for it. Broken furniture and mops and buckets.

"Storage," Ares said.

"Our lucky day." And I meant it.

"Seriously. I'd hate to break into the guards' break room."

I chuckled and slipped between two broken tables to reach the door. It was unlocked, and I slipped it open to peer outside.

The wide hallway was more formal than the storage room—very much like the entryway with its dark wood walls and fancy lighting.

I ducked back inside. "It's the main building. Decorated the same."

"Can your Seeker sense find the Master of Secrets?"

"I can try. But since I only have his title, it's very unlikely." I called upon my magic, digging deep and feeding it my desire to find the Master of Secrets.

But since it had nothing more to go on, it lay dormant.

I pushed harder, wishing to speak to him.

Nothing, nada, zip. "No luck. I'd need more info about him to get a connection. We'll have to find someone to take us there."

"No problem."

I opened the door and slipped out into the hallway, going left on a whim. Or instinct. Instinct sounded better, so I'd go with that.

The hall was wide and the navy rug beneath our feet very plush, so it was easy to keep our footsteps silent. Fortunately, we saw no one. But the sound of voices in the hallway to the left made me stiffen. They were coming closer.

A doorway on the right beckoned.

In there, I mouthed.

We ducked inside. It was a small library. From the looks of the titles, all the books had to do with law. I cracked the door and peered out. Ares crowded behind me, his strong body warm behind mine. I shivered, having to force myself to focus on the hall outside.

Five people walked by, all dressed in long navy robes. Magica, if I had to guess. Their signatures didn't feel shiftery, at least. Shifters smelled more like animals, though not usually in a bad way.

Usually.

"Too many," Ares murmured in my ear.

I shivered at the whisper of his breath. "Yeah."

We could take them, but it wouldn't be silent. And we needed silent.

Fortunately, a single pair of footsteps sounded a moment later, coming down the hall from the opposite direction.

"I've got this," Ares whispered.

I stepped back, letting him have the position closest to the crack in the door. As the footsteps neared, he tensed. When they were right by us, Ares swung the door open and darted out into the hallway, grabbing the figure and pulling him inside.

The man was only about five and a half feet tall and looked a bit like a weasel, with pinched features and beady black eyes. Those eyes were wild over the hand that Ares had clamped over his mouth.

I shut the door behind them as Ares dragged the man into the center of the room. A letter opener on the desk caught my eye, and I grabbed it, then approached the pair.

"We're looking for the Master of Secrets," I said. "We'd like you to tell us where he is."

The man frantically shook his head.

"That's a no, I think." I looked at Ares.

He nodded.

"We could convince you." I held up the letter opener.

"Scream and I'll kill you." Ares removed his hand from the man's mouth.

"That's just a letter opener," the man spat.

I shrugged. "It'll still pierce your jugular if I try hard enough. I'm willing to give it my all." I *really* hoped he bought what I was selling.

The man whitened.

Jackpot. "Now tell us where the Master of Secrets is. We just want to ask questions."

"Never. We're surrounded by my brothers and sisters. You're no threat to me."

I strode to him and pressed the tip of the blade against his neck. I pushed hard enough to hurt, but not enough to break the skin. "You see this collar around my throat?"

The man nodded, his dark eyes bulging like a frightened rat's.

"This collar means I'm dead in thirty-six hours unless I get to speak to your Master. So trust me when I say I've got nothing to lose and am willing to kill you in a building where I'm surrounded by your henchmen."

It was a bluff. I couldn't stab an innocent guy in the neck. But I gave it my best Voldemort impression. Something in my expression must have convinced him. Or maybe it was the fact that I pressed on the knife until a bead of blood welled. It was as far as I was willing to go, so I was glad it worked.

"Fine—fine," he stammered. "The Master of Secrets is at the end of this hall, then left. His office is the last door on the right."

"Thanks. Is he there now?"

The man nodded frantically. "Should be. Yes. Yes."

I debated asking him to take us there, but if we saw anyone else, he could signal for help. I looked at Ares. "Can you put him to sleep?"

The man's dark eyes flared. Ares gripped his throat and did that strange sleeper thing I needed to learn. Our rat went limp, and Ares caught him.

"Behind the desk." I hurried to the windows and tore off the ties that held the draperies back, then went to the man and bound his hands and feet. A gag finished the job. "That should buy us some time."

Ares went to the door and peered out. "Come on."

I followed him out of the room and down the hall. We sprinted on silent feet toward the next turn, pulling up short to peer around the corner.

Fortunately, there was no one coming, so we raced toward the last door on the right, which was shut.

Ares opened it and we strode inside the large office. Card catalogues sat against the wall, and there was a big desk in the middle, right in front of windows overlooking the main street in front of the station.

An old man sat at the desk. He wore the same navy robes as the other men, but his had golden braiding on the shoulder.

His eyes widened, and he surged to his feet. "Who are you?"

"I'm Phoenix Knight, and this is Ares Warhaven. We're here to ask you about Marin Olerafort."

Understanding dawned on the man's face, and he looked at Ares. "You are the Enforcer of the Vampire Court." His gaze moved to me. "Though I don't know who you are."

"Just the way I like it." I pulled the medallion out of my pocket and held it up. "Marin Olerafort was murdered, and we're looking for the killer. He had one of these, and it led us here."

"You think the murder has something to do with us?" he asked.

"I don't know what this place is exactly, or who you are. But you're secretive. And one of your men referred to his colleagues here as his brothers and sisters. That means you're close to each other." *Or a weird cult.* "We're hoping that you cared for Marin as much as Ares did and that you'll help us solve the mystery of his death."

Ares's gaze shifted to mine and stuck. Did he think I didn't realize he cared for Marin?

Dudes and hiding their feelings.

The Master of Secrets sighed, then sat. He gestured to two chairs in front of us. "You may as well have a seat."

"Thank you." I sat. Ares joined me, taking the other chair.

"What is this place?" Ares asked. "Marin worked for us in the Vampire Court, but we didn't realize he had a side job."

"It's not a job. More of a calling. Informas assist us as their time permits them to." The Master of Secrets steepled his hands together. "This is the Order of the Secret Stealers."

"Marin was an Informa?" Ares asked.

"He was. Though they frequently do not reveal themselves, even to those that care about them."

Informas. I'd heard of them before. They were a sort of supernatural who could steal information from someone's mind. I remembered the info written on the cards in the card catalogue at the top of the bell tower.

"But what do you do with the information you have?" I asked. "Do you just take it to know it?"

Like gossip hounds? What was the purpose?

He sighed. "Some of it, yes. It is our passion—to know all. But the most important secrets—those upon which the safety of supernaturals rests—those we protect."

"How?" Ares asked.

"Through a very complex spell that ensures it never gets out."

"Yikes." I leaned forward. "Does that mean you kill whoever you steal it from so that they don't know it?"

"Of course not! We aren't murderers. But it is also why the protection spell is so complex. We must compel an unknown number of individuals to never speak of the secret."

I leaned forward. "So was Marin after one of these super secrets?"

"He was. Though I do not know the nature of it."

"Did he just go after it recently?" I asked. "Right before he was killed?"

The Master of Secrets's brow crumpled, and he swallowed hard. "Yes. He left on the mission only three days ago."

"Then it's probably no coincidence that he was murdered shortly after," Ares said.

"Do you know who else might want this secret?" I asked. "Maybe they killed him for it?"

"Or they were the people he took the information from," Ares said. "They may want vengeance."

"Either is possible. Even likely," the Master of Secrets said. "We can give you the location of his last mission. I don't know what he sought there, but we often shared the location of our hunts as a safety mechanism."

"Thank you." My heart raced. This could be it. These people he was leading us to might be Marin's murderers. They might be the answer to me getting the collar off.

The Master of Secrets pulled a piece of paper from his drawer and wrote on it, then passed it across the desk. "He went to an ancient Cathar castle in Southern France. It is inhabited by Cathar Perfecti. There are coordinates on that paper. Marin worked hard to get them. But what he found there, I do not know."

"Weren't the Cathars a medieval religious sect? I thought they died out after the Catholics defeated them in their crusade. Thirteenth century, wasn't it?" I asked.

"The human Cathars did not fare well," the Master of Secrets said. "But there was one sect that survived. Supernaturals who hid themselves with powerful magic. They missed the massacre and the horror."

"Are they still hidden?" I asked. "Can we even find them?"

"They no longer use magic to hide their whereabouts because no one hunts them any longer. Magic like that costs a lot of money, and they don't have it. Anyway, their enemies are no longer in the business of crusades, so why bother?"

"But it took Marin a long time to find the place?" I asked. "Otherwise you'd have gotten your information sooner."

The Master of Secrets nodded. "They've been all but forgotten by history, thought to be dead. Now they are a quiet settlement, well guarded from uninvited guests. Or so Marin believed."

Of course they were well guarded. No way we'd be lucky enough to just walk right up to their doorstep.

"What kind of protections do they have?"

"Marin believed that it was primarily enchantments to repel humans. I can imagine they'd prefer not to have confused hikers at their door."

"Any chance you could give them a heads up we're coming?" I asked. "Peaceful visit, questions only?"

"No, I don't know them so my word will mean nothing. Marin had to navigate the dangers himself. He didn't know what to expect, as he learned of it secondhand, or he would have told me. We shared as much as we could about our missions in case we didn't return."

I glanced at Ares, quirking a brow. He nodded subtly. This was all we would get here.

We stood.

"Thank you for the help," I said.

"My pleasure." The Master of Secrets nodded. "When you achieve justice for Marin, please let me know."

I hoped I'd have some good news for him. Because if I had no news about Marin's real killer, I'd be too dead to deliver it anyway.

CHAPTER ELEVEN

Six of the "brothers" escorted us to the public exit. Three in front of us, three behind. It was billed as a polite gesture, but it was really just a way of ensuring we didn't snoop around anymore.

After the structural damage we'd caused, I couldn't blame them.

The brothers were supernaturals of all varieties, but after feeling out their magical signatures, it became clear that they all shared a particular scent to their magic. It was like old paper. Marin had smelled the same.

That must be the Informa's signature.

"So, you guys do a lot of secret hunting?" I asked as they led us down the hall toward the main door.

No one answered me.

"I'll take that as a yes."

Still, no answer. One of the three at the front opened a heavy wooden door, and we were escorted out into the familiar alley. The same one we'd tried to break in through last night.

"*This* is your public entrance?" I asked. It was so violent and dirty, what with the booby traps and homicidal guard demons that we'd encountered last night.

"We don't really want visitors." The tallest Informa said.

"Mission accomplished," I said.

He gestured down the alley. "Continue on."

They led us down the smelly corridor, past dumpsters and the places where the booby traps had gone off last night. Thankfully, there were no repeats. When we reached the end of the alley, the tallest Informa stepped forward. "This is where we leave you. Do not return."

I waved at them, but their stony gazes were hard as they disappeared back down the alley.

"That's a tough crowd," I said.

"They're certainly wary of outsiders." Ares stepped out into the sunlight of the main street.

I followed, leaving the smelly shadows of the alley behind. We had a plan. I held on to that tightly. The idea that I had less than two days left threatened to overwhelm me. Focusing on the plan helped.

Ares turned to me. "I'll transport us to—"

A small silver sphere fell out of the air and landed between us. A sonic boom threw us off our feet. I slammed into the wall behind me, pain streaking through me as my knees gave out, and I slid to the ground. Through hazy vision, I saw attackers come from either side of the alley.

They'd been waiting. Four of them.

Ares was on the ground fifteen feet away. I gasped and struggled upright, conjuring a sword and shield as a tall man in a black coat leapt for me. His magic surged around him, and he threw a fireball straight for my head.

I raised my shield. The fireball slammed into it. I peeked around my protection. My attacker was charging up another fireball, while Ares was fighting two attackers in the distance. His shadow sword swirled on the air.

I wasn't going to get this Fire Mage with a sword, so I dropped it and conjured a knife.

He threw another fireball at me, which I barely blocked. While he was charging up another, I lowered the shield and hurled my knife at him.

It sank into his neck. The flame that surrounded his palm died. He collapsed.

Guilt flared inside me as my FireSoul flared. I *hated* killing. But it had been him or me, and it wasn't going to be me. I staggered away from him, fighting the urge to steal his magic. It rose up inside me, hungry even though my stomach lurched at the idea.

A shuffling sounded from behind me. I whirled. Another attacker came at me with a sword raised. He was bigger than me and looked a hell of a lot meaner.

No big deal.

This, I could handle.

I swooped up my sword from the ground and charged him. Our blades clanged.

He pressed his sword hard against mine, as if trying to use his greater strength to force my own sword back onto me. Or force me to drop it.

Ha. As if I'd drop my sword.

I took advantage of his stupid maneuver and kicked him in the gut, then ducked low and pulled away from him. As he was recovering, I swung my blade hard for his, knocking his own from his hands.

I pressed the tip of my sword to his throat, forcing him backward until he stood against the wall.

A quick glance behind my shoulder showed that Ares had killed one of his attackers and had another—a woman—by the throat.

I turned back to the big man who'd come at me with the sword. He had a bald head and big mustache, like a carnival strongman. But the menace in his dark eyes and the tattoo of a dragon that covered his head made him look more threatening than entertaining.

His gaze darted behind me, presumably to Ares and the woman.

"Why are you trying to kill me?" I demanded.

He spat at me. I dodged, barely.

"Gross." I pressed the blade slightly harder against his throat. "I really don't mind killing you for information. Not after you tried to cut off my head."

"Do it." But his gaze darted back behind me. To Ares and the woman. Worry glittered in his eyes.

Ah.

A weak point. Just like the Monster had used with me. I felt sick using the same tactic of threatening a loved one, but I called out to Ares.

"Don't kill her!" I said. "Bring her closer."

"Fine." Ares dragged the woman closer until I could see them out of the corner of my eye.

I turned to the man. "Tell me why you're after me, or he'll kill her."

As soon as I said the words, my stomach lurched. I hated this. It was different than killing someone while protecting yourself. That was heat of the moment, kill or be killed. And I knew that there was no way I could do it. Or order Ares to do it.

"Don't!" The woman cried, her voice strangled from Ares's hand about her throat. "Do not breathe a word!"

The man's tortured gaze met hers.

"We'll kill her." I made my voice hard as stone. "My friend is a vampire and would be happy to drain her dry. Why did you attack?"

The man shot one last glance at the woman. His mouth twisted. For a moment, I thought it was with regret.

Then I realized that he'd done something I'd only ever seen in the movies. He'd used his tongue to prod at one of his teeth and released a pill of some kind. A cyanide capsule in the human world.

Whatever it was, as soon as he crunched down on it, his eyes rolled back into his head and he collapsed.

"Shit!" I jumped back, then whirled to Ares.

In his arm, the woman collapsed as well. She, too, had eaten her cyanide capsule.

"Damn it." Frantic, I looked between the two of them. "What now?"

Regret sliced Ares's face. He hoisted the woman into his arms and put her body in the alley. "Let the Order of Secret Stealers deal with them. I'll call a couple of my men here to ask questions if necessary and get any details off the bodies."

I nodded. This sucked. He may have given them info. And I hated that they'd died. I hadn't wanted to kill the man who'd thrown fireballs at me, but he'd been on the offensive seeking to kill me back.

This guy had technically been my prisoner. I didn't want him to die.

Ares returned and picked up the man as if he weighed nothing.

But the body began to disintegrate. It turned to dust, like some mummy in an old movie.

Ares jumped back, dropping the body. In the alley, the woman turned to dust as well. I glanced behind me, seeking the man in the coat who'd thrown fireballs at me.

Horrified, I pointed. "He's dusting too."

"All of them are. What the hell is it?"

"A spell. Something so that they leave no evidence." All trace of them was already gone. Damn it.

"Let's get out of here." Ares held out a hand. "We'll figure this out elsewhere. It's not safe here."

I was with him on that. I reached out a hand and grasped his. The ether sucked us in, transporting us to a busy city street that was definitely not Magic's Bend. The buildings were bigger and older and much more ornate.

"Where are we?" I let go of his hand.

"My place in Paris. Come on." Ares led me toward the entrance of the building.

Again, there was a doorman, but this one looked more like a bodyguard than anything else. He was huge, with shoulders like a mountain and a scrunched-up face.

He nodded to Ares and pulled open the door.

"Thank you, Phillipe," Ares said.

I followed him into an ornate lobby—this one done in ruby and dark wood—and up an ancient elevator.

"You sure have a lot of houses," I said.

"Only four. And this is the closest one to the Cathar castle."

The elevator stopped, and he led me out, toward a door about ten feet down the hall. He pressed his palm to the wood and magic sparked, then he pushed the door open and stepped inside.

I followed, stepping into a large living room with old windows overlooking the Eiffel Tower. It was decorated differently than his place at Magic's Bend, with heavy furniture done in creams and blue.

"What the hell was that all about?" I asked.

"No idea. They weren't after me. I just settled my last real issue of that nature."

"Then they were after me." Chills raced over my skin. I wanted to take a seat, but forced myself to toughen up.

"Any reason in particular?"

"Marin's murder. That's the only weird thing I've got going now." The Monster from our past used to hunt us, but that was over.

"Then Marin's murder is more complicated than we thought," Ares said.

I walked to the window. "Yeah. Which means they're a group,

not just one guy who killed Marin. And they're keeping themselves mighty secret with that dusting power."

"No evidence, that's for sure. Of anything."

I tried calling on my dragon sense, asking it to lead me to wherever our attackers had come from, but as expected, it didn't work.

Total shot in the dark anyway. Not enough info to go on.

"But how did they find us?"

He joined me at the window, looking out over the view of Paris's most famous landmark. "They're tracking you, or they knew you might go to the Order of Secret Stealers for information. They want to frame you."

Surprise flashed through me. I hadn't expected him to tell me that. His honesty—and trust?—warmed something inside of me.

"I know," I said. "I heard you talking last night in the hotel. Was it to the Vampire Court?"

His green gaze met mine, annoyed. "You eavesdropped?"

I pointed to the collar around my neck. "My life is at stake here. Of course I eavesdropped."

He nodded. "Fine. I'd do the same. And yes. Someone is trying to frame you. The Vampire Court is looking to find the murderer quickly, and you're their best bet. And the false accusations don't help."

"But *you're* one third of the Vampire Court!" I said. "Can't you get me off if you know I'm innocent?"

"I'm an equal third. But with the other two against me, I'm outnumbered." He propped his hands on the windowsill and leaned against it. "There's no camaraderie between myself and the other members of the Vampire Court. Magisteria and Doyen don't like each other any more than they like me. In a way, it helps. We each uphold our part of the government. It keeps us honest and truthful."

"There's never an attempt to overthrow the others?" I asked.

"I'm the only one strong enough to attempt it, and I have no interest in ruling alone. That would change the whole structure of our government. Now, I have freedom. If I overthrow Magisteria and Doyen, I become King."

"That's kinda cool."

His skeptical gaze met mine. "Hardly. Just because I have the strength to overthrow the government, doesn't mean I want to. I'd have to live in the Vampire Realm full-time, ruling my subjects." He straightened. "Frankly, I'd rather take a stake to the heart."

"Stakes are a myth." I sighed. Plenty of things could kill vampires. "But I get your point."

He wasn't going to give up his whole life for me. He might believe I hadn't committed the murder, but he wasn't going to sacrifice everything. I didn't like it, but I couldn't blame him. I wouldn't do the same for him.

"Where's your bathroom?" I asked.

"To the left, down the hall."

"Thanks." I hurried away, shutting myself inside the small guest bathroom that was fancier than everything in my apartment combined. Besides my trove, obviously.

I leaned against the wall.

Shit. This was bad. I drew in a ragged breath and called upon my dragon sense, begging it to find me Marin's killer. But I had nothing more than a shadowy figure in the dark to go on. Even my desire to find the murderer and save my own life didn't do the trick.

I needed more info.

If anything, it felt like my dragon sense tugged me south. An image of a castle flashed in my mind. The Cathar castle. That was where my dragon sense was sending me.

I didn't get it, but I had to follow. There would be answers there. I had to trust that.

I pushed away from the wall and washed my face, avoiding

looking into the mirror to see how rough I looked after a day of fighting and scrambling through ancient corridors.

Refreshed, I pressed my fingertips to the comms charm at my neck. "Cass? Del?"

"Yeah? Any luck?" Cass answered.

"We're headed to a Cathar castle in southern France, looking for answers. But will you guys do whatever research you can on a breed of supernaturals called Informas?"

"Sure thing," Del said. "Who's an Informa?"

"Marin Olerafort, the victim. And this is more than just a murder. There's something bigger at stake."

"Not bigger than your life," Cass said.

I smiled. It was good to have them at my back. "Thanks."

"Well, we're on it," Del said. "Call us if you need any more help."

"I will. Thanks, guys."

"Anytime," Cass said.

"Stay safe!" Del added.

"Will do." I cut the connection, then sucked in a deep breath and left the bathroom to rejoin Ares.

He turned from the window to face me.

"We need to get to this Cathar castle," I said. "I think we're close. That secret is tied up in all of this."

"I agree. We can go now if you're ready."

"Ready as I'll ever be."

Ares unfolded the paper that the Master of Secrets had given him and studied it.

"What's it say?"

"It's coordinates."

"You can navigate the ether using that?"

He shrugged. "Shouldn't be too hard."

"Good." I held out my hand. "Let's go."

His strong hand gripped my own, and he pulled me closer to him. My breath caught. I should be used to his nearness by now, but I wasn't. He smelled good and looked better, especially up close.

"Ready?" he asked.

Was his voice slightly rougher?

Nah. Crazy.

I nodded.

Magic sparked on the air, and the ether dragged us across the country. We appeared in southern France, at the base of a mountain topped by a castle.

I stepped back and craned my head to look up. "Whoa. They live up there?"

The mountain was steep, with dark green scrub brush along the sides.

"How the hell did they build that castle up there?" Ares asked.

"No idea. But I guess if you had to protect yourself from a crusade, you're going to build up high."

Ares nodded. "It would be easy to defend."

"That's what I'm afraid of." I sighed. "Any chance you can transport us to the top?"

"I can try."

I reached for his hand, holding tight. The ether pulled at us, sucking us in again. My heart leapt. This might work! I opened my eyes.

We were a couple hundred yards up the mountain, but no farther. Dang.

"Their protective magic won't let me go any farther," Ares said.

"Then let's get started. That mountain isn't going to climb itself."

We began the hike, scrambling over the scrub brush and eventually finding a worn path. The mountain wasn't super tall, but it was steep. One side of the path rose sharply upward toward the castle; the other plummeted down to a ravine.

I estimated an hour's climb if we got lucky.

I sure hoped we got lucky. The sun was turning the sky pink as it neared the horizon. Darkness wouldn't help our cause.

As we trekked upward and my breathing became rough, I vowed to lay off the cheese and hit the gym.

I couldn't help the laugh that escaped.

"What are you laughing about?" Ares asked.

"Um, nothing interesting." *Just my long-lived affair with cheddar.*

Magic sparked on the air, and the ground rumbled, distracting him.

"Something is coming," he said.

I glanced around. A half second later, a trio of large rocks tumbled down the mountain toward us. Gravel slid alongside.

"Rockfall!" I cried.

We sprinted forward as the rocks tumbled onto the path. Dust flew up behind me, creating a haze that clouded the air. I kept close to Ares's heels, sprinting with everything I had.

A glance upward revealed a massive boulder about to land right on us. There was a tall, shallow cave to our left, right in the mountainside. It was more of an indention in the rock wall, but it was the only shelter around, and our only hope.

"Ares!" I cried, then hurled myself into him with the last of my strength, pushing him toward the cave.

We slammed against the back wall of the shallow cave just as the boulder slammed onto the path where we'd been standing.

It trapped us inside, leaving just a sliver of space at the edge where light could filter in.

"Holy hell." Ares's wide gaze was on the boulder. "You saved us."

I panted, my body pressed hard to his. Adrenaline surged through me. My limbs shook, and my heart raced.

I glanced up at him, painfully aware of how close we were. How good he felt, pressed against me. I was selective about the guys I dated—which meant I dated mostly fictional dudes in my head.

This was the first time in ages I'd been so close to a guy in a dark—um, room?—and Ares... Well, he was the hottest, strongest guy I'd ever met.

It was hard not to like that. A lot. Even when I knew it was stupid, I liked it.

His green gaze met mine. A slash of light cut across his face, making his eyes glitter.

I'd have bet anything that there was hunger in his gaze. When his hand pressed against my lower back, cementing me to him, I knew it. Definitely hunger.

For me.

I drew in an unsteady breath, goosebumps prickling my skin as warmth welled inside me. My gaze dropped to his lips, which looked so full and kissable I could lose my mind any second.

"Nix." His voice was rough. Wanting.

Oh my fates, he was going to kiss me. Right on the lips.

It snapped me out of my trance.

I didn't have time for this. *Literally* did not have time for it if I wanted to keep on living.

I cleared my throat and pulled away. I could only step back a foot before I collided with the boulder that trapped us.

But the space was enough to clear my head. It seemed to clear his as well, because he straightened and his businesslike mask fell back over his face. "I'll get us out of here."

"Yeah." My voice was an embarrassing croak. "Good idea."

I squeezed myself into the corner so he had room to work.

He pressed his hands against the rock. The thing had to weigh several tons at least. But he pushed it like it was a feather. He didn't even grimace. Just...*shoved.*

The boulder disappeared down the mountain. From what I could hear, it crushed anything in its path, and I was sure glad it wasn't me.

I eyed him appreciatively. "So that's what vampire strength is."

"Yes." He leaned out of the cave and looked both directions. "The rockfall has settled down."

"If I were a hiker, I'd have headed back in the other direction."

"Same."

"Onward?"

He nodded. "Onward."

We continued to climb. Despite the chill air, sweat began to dampen my skin. The sky turned a darker orange as the sun dipped below the horizon.

"Halfway there," Ares said.

I wanted to answer, but I was too busy trying not to breathe like a couch potato forced to run a 10K.

A whistling noise cut through the air.

My brain registered the threat—arrow!—just as Ares grabbed me around the waist and threw me to the ground. His body landed on top of mine, protecting me.

He grunted, a sound of obvious pain.

I called upon my magic, conjuring a long shield.

"Come on, get behind this!" I said.

We scrambled behind the shield, crouching low as arrows thudded against it. An arrow was stuck in Ares's arm, fully piercing the muscle of his bicep.

I winced. "Ouch."

"No kidding." He grimaced, then snapped the feathers off the arrow and pulled it through the hole in his arm. After that initial grimace, he didn't even flinch.

Yikes. I wondered what pain he'd felt in the past that made it so he didn't flinch when an arrow went straight through his arm.

It must not be easy being the vampire Enforcer.

I peeked around the side of the shield, getting the briefest glimpse of arrows flying out of the narrow windows in the castle's three towers.

"Hey!" Ares grabbed my shoulder and yanked me back. "You need to be more careful."

I scowled at him.

"Come on," he said. "You have to admit that sticking your head out when arrows are flying at us is dumb."

"Fine. It is. But I wanted to know where they are coming from."

"The towers, right?"

"Yes. But I saw a man, too, standing at the top of one of the towers."

"That is useful." His brow furrowed. "Could you conjure a white flag that he could see?"

"Think they'd get it?" I asked. "Is that a universal sign of surrender or just something in movies?"

"Can't hurt to try."

"Yeah, okay." I hadn't done too much conjuring today, so I had a good store of power saved up.

As the arrows thudded against our shield, I conjured a white cloth. Ares tied it to a stick, then hoisted it in the air. We waited, breath held.

CHAPTER TWELVE

Finally, the arrows stopped.

A voice echoed down the mountain. It took me a moment to recognize it as French, though a strange older version. "Who are you?"

"Not Crusaders!" I yelled back in his language.

Ares glanced at me, brow raised.

I shrugged. "That's who they're scared of."

"You speak French?"

"I'm pretty good at languages. Lots of study time behind the desk at Ancient Magic. Do you understand him?"

"Yes. Though my French is very rusty. Let's leave the talking to you."

"Approach!" the voice shouted.

"That's only somewhat promising," Ares said. "They could still drop boiling oil on our heads as soon as we get to the gate."

"These guys may have been the ones to kill Marin, so I'd say it's more probable than possible."

"It's our only option, though. Let's take the shield and see what they have up their sleeve. My instinct is that they didn't murder Marin, so we'd be better off with a truce."

"Okay. I just hope you're right."

We crept out from behind the shield. Ares took it from me and held it out in front of us. The man on top of the castle was dressed in brown robes. He was thin as an arrow, but I couldn't tell anything else from this distance.

The rest of the walk was uneventful, despite the fact that my heart raced the entire time, and I didn't stop looking for arrows.

When we reached the heavy wooden gate, we kept back, far enough away that any boiling oil wouldn't splash on us. The gate stayed firmly shut.

I leaned back and looked up. The castle wall rose tall above me. The man in the brown robe leaned over the ramparts forty feet above. His face was broad and plain, with brown hair and eyes that were an identical shade. He didn't look like a murderer. But then, they often didn't

"Who are you?" he shouted.

If they were the murderers and they'd framed me, I didn't want to give them my name.

"I am Caroline Farrow and this is—" I hesitated, mind racing. "This is Kevin Petergrass. We're here with questions about a man who recently took information from you."

The man scowled, then disappeared back behind the wall.

"Do you think he's consulting his buddies?" I asked Ares.

"Probably."

"I vow not to use magic against you!" I shouted. "I'm just a Conjurer anyway!"

The man leaned back over the castle wall. "You are not just a Conjurer."

I winced. Ares gave me a *told you so* look.

"But I really mean you no harm!" I said.

"That, I believe. We will allow you in to ask your questions, but if you use any magic, we will toss you off the castle wall."

Not very peaceable, but okay. It was all I was going to get. "Thanks!"

The gate groaned as it lifted.

"Kevin Petergrass?" Ares whispered to me.

"It was all I could think of in the moment. I don't think they would have liked *Ares Warhaven*. And if they've been hiding out here for a millennia, then they don't know who you are."

"I hope you're right."

"Do you think they did it?"

"Maybe. But if so, we won't have any trouble against some old monks."

Fair enough.

The gate lifted to reveal a cluster of men, all dressed in identical brown robes. There were twelve of them, and they looked like monks, but the Master of Secrets had called them Perfecti. I sensed a few different magical signatures, but they weren't prominent.

The man who'd stood at the top of the castle wall stepped forward. "You may enter."

"Thank you." My heart thundering, I stepped in alongside Ares, who looked nothing like a Kevin Petergrass.

I sure hoped Ares was right and these guys weren't the murderers.

Dark had fallen, and flickering torches shed a golden glow over the barren courtyard. Three benches were the only objects in the small space. The castle itself was cramped, the three towers butting up to the small open area in the middle. Not a lot of room on top of a mountain, apparently.

And we were the first interesting thing they'd seen in a while, from the way their gazes were riveted to us.

Actually, scratch that. They looked annoyed.

"We're here to ask questions about the man who stole information from you." I wasn't going to mention that Marin had been ol' Kevin Petergrass's buddy.

"You mean the *men* who stole from us."

My gaze darted to Ares's. He shrugged just slightly.

"There was more than one?" I asked.

The Perfecti nodded, then gestured us inside. "Come, we will take a seat."

I frowned at Ares, not wanting to go deeper into their castle. Ares nodded encouragingly. We'd faced worse odds and come out all right.

He led us across the courtyard toward the back tower. The other Perfecti followed, a silent mass.

Oh, more bad puns.

Were they there to guard us or because we were entertainment in an otherwise quiet life? My skin chilled. Or perhaps they wanted revenge on their stolen secret? But they didn't know that Ares had been friends with Marin.

The room that we entered was in the base of one of the three towers. It was almost as barren as the courtyard, with two simple trestle tables made of wood. There wasn't even a fireplace, and it was barely warmer in here than it had been outside.

These Perfecti were really committed to their ascetic lifestyle.

The leader gestured to the table, and we sat on one bench. He sat across from us. The others stood by the wall. Watching.

"What do you want to know?" he asked.

"You mentioned that there were two men here?" I asked.

"Yes. An older man and a younger one. They came to steal one of our most carefully guarded secrets."

"What was it?" Ares asked.

The Perfecti raised both brows in an expression that so clearly said, *Are you kidding me, Kevin?*

Ares raised his hands. "Forget I asked. Could you please tell us about the younger man? What was he doing here?"

"He looked like he was fighting with the older one. Both attempted to steal information from our vault. Only one succeeded—the older man. We came upon them in a scuffle in the vault. Our attack... We are rusty after so many years. They both got away."

"Could you tell us anything about the younger man?" I begged. "Anything at all. We want to find him. And I vow, when we do, whatever secret he stole, will die with him."

Okay, maybe I was laying it on a little thick there. But the Perfecti seemed to appreciate it. He smiled, and it was just a bit bloodthirsty.

"What about the older man?" he asked. "Do you not care about him?"

"He is dead." Ares's voice was hard. But it was the kind of hard that hid pain. I knew that voice. My *deirfiúr* and I used it on occasion. "We want vengeance on his killer."

"The younger man?" the leader guessed.

"Yes," I said.

The man nodded, understanding glinting in his eyes. "If you kill both, the secret dies with them."

"Provided that they didn't pass it on," I said, trying for honesty that might endear me to them.

Satisfaction glinted in the leader's eyes. "It is very hard to interpret our information. They stole the information—but it is in code. Some words recognizable, others not. They will have an inkling of the information we sought to protect, but not enough to do damage. They would need more time to understand it. Weeks, months, years, depending upon how clever they are. If you catch him quickly, it will be all right."

I grinned. "Then if you tell us what you know of the younger man, I vow that we will make sure the secret dies with him."

Or the Vampire Court would make sure it died with him. I'd be off the hook, back to my normal life.

"We can do better than that." The leader raised a hand, gesturing to one of the other men. "Please bring the fabric."

"What fabric?" Ares asked.

"In the scuffle, we stole a piece of his cloak. It had initials sewn into it. And we have an Illusory here. He can play back a past event so that you can see what the man looked like."

My heart raced. An object linked to the man, plus a view of his face? That should spark my dragon sense. Objects were often the most helpful. This is what I'd been missing in my attempts to track him.

"Thank you," I said.

A man stepped forward—the Illusory, I presumed. "We must go to the scene of the theft," he said. "There, I will call up the past."

Too bad we couldn't interact with it. Del could bring the past back and interact with it, but it was deadly dangerous.

We followed the monks from the tower and through a corridor. A small doorway led to a dark staircase. I peered down as two of the Perfecti drew torches off the walls. They led the way, with Ares and me in the middle of the pack.

If I'd been claustrophobic, this tiny spiral staircase built deep into a mountain would have set me off like a firework. It was narrow, and the stone steps were so old that they were worn down to slick, slanted surfaces.

The room that we entered was tiny, with just one large book on a pedestal. That's where they kept their secrets? Good thing they were hard to interpret.

"We can fight when we need to," the Lead Perfecti said. "To protect the information in this book, we do fight. But the man who stole from us was quick and clever. He came with magic that we weren't prepared for."

"And we've grown a bit out of practice these long years," another Perfecti said.

The leader shot him a sharp glare. He stared right back, hard as stone.

I so did not want to get in the middle of a fight between those two.

The Illusory stepped forward, raising his hands like he was going to conduct an orchestra. Magic fizzled on the air, and two figures appeared. They were shimmery at first, then coalesced until they looked as real as if we were here with them.

Marin stood over the book, reading from the pages. His long cloak fell from his shoulders to the floor. The younger man crept up from behind, his footsteps silent. I wanted to shout to Marin, but knew it would do no good.

The attacker raised a knife that had been hidden in his cloak. I thought he'd plunge it into Marin's back, but at the last moment, Marin turned.

"Aleric!" Surprise echoed in Marin's voice. He shot out his hand, sending a blast of wind at his opponent.

The man flew back against the wall.

I whirled to catch sight of his face.

Middle-aged, black hair, blue eyes. Scar across the chin and a nose with the tip missing. I imprinted it on my memory, studying every little detail that I could. As he charged Marin, his cloak flew back from his chest to reveal a tattoo at the base of his neck.

A dragon.

Just like the big man from the attack at Saint Pancras.

Just before the attacker reached Marin, the Perfecti ran into the room. Images of them, at least. They were part of the Illusory's spell, and were armed with swords and axes. They weren't bad with their weapons, though a bit rusty, like the one had said. Marin escaped only because of his impressive control over wind.

He blasted the Perfecti out of the way and raced up the stairs, cloak flapping behind him. The other man had a harder time. He barely escaped, but not before one of the Perfecti tore off part of his cloak.

In the real world, the Illusory gestured, and the scene disappeared.

The leader stepped forward and handed me a scrap of cloak. "Does that help?"

I held my breath and called on my dragon sense, keeping my signature repressed. I begged it to find the man who owned this cloak, picturing his face in my mind and the tattoo at his neck. And his name. Aleric.

My dragon sense latched on.

Yes.

"That helps," I whispered. Armed with a name, a face, and a piece of his clothing—now my dragon sense had enough that it could not fail.

"Then catch him," the leader said. "Catch him and deliver justice."

"Oh, I will." And I'd save myself as well.

Ares transported us back to Magic's Bend, directly to Ancient Magic. It'd taken some convincing, but he'd agreed when I'd explained that I wanted to confer with my *deirfiúr* and see if they'd learned anything about the Informas. Plus, we'd need their help.

Because of the time change, it was nearly sunset by the time we arrived. It was a few minutes past closing time, and the shop's lights were darkened and there was no one within.

"Where do you think they are?" Ares asked. "If we can't find them, we can always bring in my men. Which I believe we should do anyway. More backup is always good."

"Agreed, though they're not as strong as my *deirfiúr*."

"That's some tough friends you've got."

"You have no idea." I glanced down the street toward P & P. "And at this hour on a Friday, I know just where they are."

"Lead on."

I started down the street, Ares at my side. The streetlamps flickered on as dusk settled. The silence was heavy—unusual for us. Not that we were chatty, but there was something else in the air. Almost...sadness.

I'd never been able to sense things like that before, but there was a first time for everything.

"Are you thinking about Marin?" I asked.

Ares hesitated. When he spoke, his voice was just a bit rough. "Yes."

"You were close."

"We were." He hesitated again, as if speaking like this was uncomfortable.

Come on... I wanted to poke him until more information fell out. I wanted to know more about him, even if it might make me like him more. Because any information about an opponent was good, right?

But was he still my opponent?

This collar said yes.

Ares sighed. "Later in life, he was like a surrogate father to me. He helped my Enforcers, and me, with our work. I'm the only vampire who can walk in the light. As such, we need other species for business that only occurs during daylight hours."

"And Marin did that?"

"Yes. And he became a close friend."

"You played chess with him," I guessed, remembering the chess set in his apartment.

"I did."

We reached P & P. Through the glass, I could see my friends sitting in their usual spot in the ring of comfy chairs in the corner. Even Roarke, Del's boyfriend, was there. He must have finished his work in the Underworld.

I stopped, looking up at Ares.

"And you miss Marin," I said.

His eyes darkened. "I find that I do. And I want vengeance."

"We'll get it." I liked his loyalty.

"And we'll get that collar off you," he said. "But I still want to know what you are. There's a lot more you're not telling me, Nix."

I shrugged, trying to look like I thought he was suspicious for no reason. "I still don't know what you're talking about."

Before he could answer, I pushed the door open and joined my friends in the corner of P & P. It was busy on a Friday night, with Connor and Claire both working behind the bar.

Cass and Aidan sat in their usual comfy chairs, with Del and Roarke next to them. Roarke, with his black hair and eyes and *don't bother trying it* demeanor, looked like a proper Warden of the Underworld. It was a tough job, but he was suited for it. He kept the peace between the Kings of Hell, and acted as an intermediary between the Underworld and Earth's magical governments.

He was a good guy to have on our side, and Del was hardcore smitten with him. And he with her.

"Hey, guys," I said.

"Hey," Cass and Del said in unison. Roarke and Aidan got their greetings in slightly behind.

"Did you find out anything helpful?" Cass asked.

"Yeah, thank fates." I gestured to Ares. "But first, some introductions."

Ares made the rounds, introducing himself first to my *deirfiúr*, who gave him suspicious looks.

"We're not letting you take Nix back to your Vampire Court," Del said.

"Just so you're aware," Cass added.

Ares nodded, but didn't say anything. What could he say, anyway? He turned to Aidan and Roarke. "It's been a while."

"You know each other?" I asked.

"Not well. We've met once," Aidan said.

I had to imagine it was through Aidan's security business or his limited involvement with the Alpha Council.

"Twice for us," Roarke said. "Both through work."

"But we second Del and Cass's sentiments," Aidan said. "You won't take Nix to your Vampire Court."

Annoyance flashed in Ares's eyes.

Shit. Apparently he'd bite his tongue once, but maybe not twice. I grabbed his hand, squeezing hard. The action surprised me. What was I hoping to do? Control him?

Yeah right.

Ares only said, "It is not fully in my control. But I'm committed to proving Nix's innocence."

It was the best I could hope for. I glanced at him, but his gaze remained on Roarke and Aidan.

Fortunately, everyone seemed satisfied with that. Even better, Claire arrived to break the tension.

"What'll you have?" she asked Ares and me. Her British accent was as thick as Connor's.

I turned to her. She was still dressed in her fighting leathers, but had tied a black apron on top. Fortunately, her clothes were blood-free. "Did you just get off a job?"

She nodded. "Failed though. Another merc nabbed the bounty. So I'll finish the night helping Connor." She grinned. "Pay's not as good, but it's less deadly."

Her brother was behind the bar, quickly filling drinks, though not quickly enough. There was a line of supernaturals eagerly awaiting their weekend fuel.

"Thanks for coming over," I said. "Could I have a latte and whatever cheesy thing you have left over from today? A pasty or whatever?"

Claire and Connor were from Cornwall original, home of the Cornish pasty. Food was usually only a simple breakfast and lunch thing here. Easy things that could be made in their small kitchen, and the pasty fit the bill. The savory delicacies were Cass's favorite, but I liked them too.

"Sure thing." Claire looked at Ares. "And you, handsome?"

"A coffee," Ares said. "Black. And a pasty if you have another."

Claire nodded and hurried off, weaving expertly through the crowd.

"Coffee on a Friday night?" Cass said. "Must be a fight coming up. You found your murderer?"

"Yeah." I sat in one of the six plush chairs, immediately feeling every bit of my exhaustion from the day. I should've ordered a boost with my coffee. Connor specialized in adding unique potions to the coffees that would give you a bit of extra magical energy.

"Who is he?" Del asked.

"And where is he?" Cass added.

"Aleric. Member of some group of folks with dragon tattoos. And he's in Magic's Bend."

"Dragon tattoos?" Aidan asked.

"Ever heard of a group with those?" Ares asked.

"I haven't," Aidan said.

"Neither have I," Roarke said.

For some reason, it annoyed me that these jerks had dragon tattoos. I might be a FireSoul, but it wasn't like I owned dragons. But it kinda felt like they were sullying something really cool with their lame criminal shenanigans.

"Well, they're dedicated to their cause. Two committed suicide rather than submit to questioning," Ares said.

I leaned forward. "And after they died, their bodies turned to dust."

Aidan's brows rose. "That's an expensive spell. But a good one, if you don't want anyone learning from your corpse."

"Yeah. It was annoying." They might have had wallets with info or cells with valuable contacts.

"So this Aleric lives somewhere in Magic's Bend," Cass said. "We can go get him. The six of us. Tonight."

Her quick offer of support made me grin. I'd expected it, because it's just how we operated, but I still liked hearing it. "Not sure if he actually lives here, but he's here now for some reason."

"We should go later." Del glanced toward the window, where people strolled by, probably on their way to the Flying Wizard, the only other bar on this street. "It's busy now. Better to go when there are less people around."

"And he may have less backup if it's late at night," Ares said.

"Good plan. And I might even get a two-hour nap in," I said. My tired bones rejoiced.

"Yeah, you look like hell warmed over," Cass said.

I grabbed one of the magazines on the little table next to me and chucked it at her. She laughed and batted it out of the way.

"But it is a good idea," Del said. "You need to recoup your power. Better than going into battle at half strength."

We'd fought our fair share of battles in all kinds of conditions, so I couldn't help but agree.

"We'll rest for a couple hours," Ares said. "Then we'll go at midnight. By the time we find Aleric, it should be late enough that the town is quiet and he's hopefully alone."

It was a solid plan. I liked recon and adventure. A change from my time in the shop. It'd almost be fun if my life didn't depend on it.

"Delivery!" Claire appeared at my chair with a tray, then set down cups and plates.

"Thank you." The words had hardly left my mouth before I dug in. After swallowing a bite of cheese and potato pasty, I looked at Cass and Del. "Did you learn anything about Informas? How they work?"

Cass nodded. "According to Dr. Garriso, they don't normally kill to get the information they want. If they touch someone, they can suck it right out of their head using their magic. And they can interpret any language."

"That's useful," Ares said.

"Very," Cass said. "It takes a lot out of them, though, especially if they're less experienced Informas. But here's something interesting—if one Informa kills another, he will inherit all of the secrets that the other possesses."

I leaned back in my chair. "Huh. That may be why Aleric

killed Marin. He wasn't able to get the secret at the Cathar castle, so he killed Marin for it."

"It works out nicely. Very neat. Logical." A thoughtful glint entered Ares's eyes. "I'll be right back."

He rose and went outside, then disappeared.

"That was a quick getaway," Del said.

"Only strong vampires can transport." Aidan looked toward the window. "And that guy qualifies."

"Is he giving you any trouble?" Roarke asked.

"Besides the collar?" I shook my head. "Nah. Not much. He doesn't know what I am, but he's suspicious."

"That's not good," Cass said. "He's government."

"Not ours, at least," Del said.

"No, but the Vampire Court would do well to curry favor with the Order of the Magica." I leaned forward and whispered. "Turning in a known FireSoul would go a long way toward that."

"We won't let it come to that," Aidan said.

"Thanks, guys." I leaned forward, propping my elbows on my knees. "But hopefully this will be over soon, and I'll never see him again."

"Knock on wood." Del knocked on her head.

I followed suit. I wasn't superstitious like she was, but she got pissed if you didn't appease the jinxing gods.

"You look a bit bummed, actually." Cass gasped. "Oh my gosh. Will you miss him?"

"No." I scowled at her. "He's put my life at risk by snapping this collar on me. No way I every want to see him again."

Lie.

Cass and Del shot me identical skeptical looks.

Fortunately, Ares returned at that moment, distracting them. Not that I was happy to see him. Nope. I was just ready for a nap.

"Any news?" I asked. "That's what you went for, right?"

"Yes. I've told some of my Enforcers to meet us at midnight, here. And I've told the Vampire Court what you've discovered about Aleric."

My heart leapt. "Will they take the collar off me early?"

"They've agreed to temporarily disable the magic, which has been done remotely. When you report to them tomorrow night, at the end of the three day period, we'll remove it."

"So at least it won't blow my head off if the magic is disabled." My chest squeezed tight. I didn't want to appear in front of the Court. "Isn't there a way to get it off without seeing them?"

"No." Ares frowned. "It's part of the collar's design. All three must touch it to remove it. It seemed like a good idea when we built it. Now, I'm not so sure."

Damn. Double damn. But I smiled and nodded, trying not to reveal the mini freak-out happening within me. "Okay, sure."

I stood. "I'm going to go get some rest. We'll head out at midnight."

"I'll walk you to your door," Ares said.

"It's okay."

"Better safe than sorry." He stood.

"Fine, but you're not coming up."

Cass and Del grinned. I scowled at them, then turned for the door. Ares followed.

The night was cold and dark as we made our way out. I couldn't wait for a nap.

"We're close," Ares said. "Thanks to you."

I pointed to the collar. "Just trying to save my own hide."

"You want justice for Marin too. I can see that."

I shrugged. "I don't like murderers. And Marin seemed like a good guy. He was trying to protect that secret by taking it, according to the Order of Secret Stealers. Do you believe that?"

"Yes. I'm good at sensing a liar. And Marin's intentions were good. He was likely sent to the Cathar castle to protect the secret from Aleric. And he almost did."

"But Aleric killed him." I clenched my fists. "I wonder what's so important and deadly."

"I don't know. But maybe we'll find out when we catch Aleric."

We reached the green door leading to my apartment. I turned to Ares. "I hate this collar, you know."

"I know. I'm sorry."

My brows rose. "I wasn't expecting an apology from you. You don't seem like the sort."

"I can be." The corner of his mouth quirked up in a grin that was devastating to my good sense. I suddenly wanted to kiss him, and that was just plain stupid. I pressed myself back against the door, moving farther away from temptation.

"You're special, Nix. More than anyone I've ever met."

I opened my mouth to deny it, but something silver flashed out of the corner of my eye. A little sphere. I'd barely registered what it was by the time it exploded. The sonic blast threw Ares and me sideways. I fell, hitting my head on the stone stoop of the next door down. Pain flared.

The last thing I saw through my fading vision was Ares, sprawled on the ground ten feet away, and six figures running toward us.

I didn't recognize a single one.

CHAPTER THIRTEEN

Pain shot through my skull as I opened my eyes. My vision was blurred, revealing only shadows and massive shapes. But I was definitely indoors. And tied to a chair. My wrists were bound behind me with thick rope.

If the soreness in my shoulders was any indication, I'd been here a little while. My feet weren't bound, which was a blessing. It kept the panic from overwhelming me.

I shifted my wrists uncomfortably, feeling a new metal bracelet around one wrist.

That wasn't mine. I wasn't big on jewelry.

Shit. It could be a concealment charm so that my friends couldn't find me. Immediately, I called my magic to me, attempting to conjure a blade but I was so woozy from the head wound that it was impossible.

I needed to get it together enough to conjure a blade. I didn't have a lot of magic left, but I should be able to manage that. I drew in an unsteady breath and blinked, trying not to move my head too much as I took in my surroundings.

A warehouse. Or a factory.

And Ares was nowhere to be found. What had happened to him?

The ceiling soared four stories above me, with wrought iron stairs in the corners leading up to a walkway built around the walls of the building, about fifteen feet in the air. There were more stairs leading up to higher walkways, as if factory overseers had liked to walk up high, surveying the workers down below.

Massive pieces of rusted iron machinery crouched along the walls of the huge space. They looked like steam machinery, so this place likely hadn't been used since the nineteenth century.

This had to be one of the abandoned factories in my neighborhood that had never been revitalized.

"Aleric!" a masculine voice shouted. "She's awake!"

Shit. That was enough recon. And my head was feeling clearer. I needed to get the hell out of here.

Unfortunately, a dozen men drifted out of the shadows that surrounded me. Then another dozen. An even twenty-four. Most had been leaning against the machinery, if I had to guess, snoozing until I woke up.

They circled me like hyenas, keeping their distance.

I caught a variety of magical signatures. There had to be at least a couple Fire Mages, an Ice Mage, several demons, and who knew what else among the motley crew. A few had the dragon tattoos, but I'd bet more had them underneath their clothes.

Losers like these didn't deserve the dragon as their symbol. And who the heck were these guys, anyway?

"Aleric!" I called. "Come out and chat!"

Carefully, I tried calling on my magic again. This time, I was able to focus and it worked. A tiny blade appeared in my hand. If I were careful, I could saw my way out of these bonds without anyone noticing.

Fortunately, none of them seemed to notice the little blade appear, but as soon as I started sawing away at the thick rope, I realized it was going to take a hell of a long time.

I kept at it, eyeing the man nearest me. He was slight, with a mean face and magic that smelled like old socks. *Ew.* I did *not* want to know what his gift was.

I met his muddy brown gaze. "Enjoying your sausage party?"

"Bitch." He spat on the ground.

"Why thank you." I fluttered my lashes at him. "Now where's your pal Aleric? I'd like to chat." And jump his ass as soon as I got out of these bonds.

"He's coming. Said to call him when you woke."

"Good. I'd like to see if he wants to play target practice with me."

Little Man gave me a dull look.

"He's the target," I clarified.

"But you're tied up."

"My friends will be here any minute." At least, I hoped they'd be. "So no, I won't always be tied up."

As I sawed at my bonds, I eyed the rest of the men. They stared at me, some with hunger in their gazes, some with violence. Only a few were apathetic. I guess I was the main entertainment? And why the hell was I here?

Sweat beaded on my skin despite the chill in the air, and I didn't like the sign of weakness. But these dudes looked shifty as hell. If I'd been free, I wouldn't have been quite so nervous. Tied up? That was another story.

At least they didn't approach.

A metal door slammed in the distance. The noise came from behind me. I tucked the blade in my palm and stopped my progress, which was painfully slow.

"Aleric?" I called. "That you, taking your sweet time?"

Just like my friends were doing.

"Anxious to see me?" The voice was more pleasant than I'd have expected from a murderer.

But then, all kinds of folks committed murder.

I craned my neck. A man approached. Middle-aged, black

hair, blue eyes. Scar across the chin and a nose with the tip missing.

Just like I'd memorized.

"Good of you to join me," I said.

"I'd have thought it was the other way around." He strolled to stop in front of me.

I immediately began sawing at my bindings again, keeping the movements tiny.

"Nah." I shook my head. "This was all part of my plan to catch you."

"Catch me?" He scoffed. "I caught *you*."

"No. That's just what it looks like. Fortunately for me, you're wrong." He'd be wrong if I could get through these damn bindings or if my friends would show up.

"Do you even know why you're here?" he demanded, clearly annoyed with my lack of fear.

"I figure you want to try to frame me for the murder of Marin Olerafort. How close am I?"

His silence confirmed it. With him this close, I was able to sense his magic. It smelled like rotten fish and sulfur. Ugh. Beneath it all, there was the slightest hint of a papery smell. I breathed shallowly through my mouth, trying to avoid the awful scent of dark magic. This guy was evil to his core. He might be an Informa, but he was something else as well.

I'd almost guess he'd been enchanted, but his gaze was too clear. He knew what he was doing.

"What's with the dark magic stink on you?" I asked. If I had to bet, his soul was rotten. But that was just superstition. "Is that why you killed Marin Olerafort? Couldn't help yourself?"

His eyes flashed. "I killed Marin Olerafort because I wanted to. Because the old fool was in my way and slowed me down."

"Bastard." Rage burned away the chill of fear. He'd *liked* killing Marin. "You enjoyed it."

It made my stomach lurch.

"Sure I enjoyed it. Everyone needs a hobby." His gaze turned dark. "And no one takes from me."

"He got to that secret before you did. Fair and square." I shook my head, disgusted. "You're pathetic. Murder. Just for a secret?"

He laughed, not seeming to mind being called pathetic. "A secret? It's more than a secret. It *changes everything.*"

The conviction in his voice made me nervous. What was the secret that Marin had died for? Clearly, it was worth a lot.

My fists itched to punch Aleric, but I wasn't through my bindings yet. "Quit being so cryptic and spill the beans. What's *everything?*"

This guy was grossing me out *and* driving me nuts.

"That's up to my Master to determine."

"Who the heck is your Master?" I looked around. "Boss man of all these fine folks?"

"You're not fit to speak his name."

"All right, then. So you're just a minion."

"Happy to play my part in something as big as this." He grinned. "As you'll play yours. In about thirty seconds, when the Vampire Court shows up."

For the first time, real, true fear chilled my bones. I froze solid in the chair, a deer in headlights. "They don't leave their realm."

"They would when I promised them Marin Olerafort's murderer."

"Not all of them." I had Ares on my side. Though I didn't know where he was.

"Two of them, though. A majority."

Shit. He was really taking this framing thing to the next level. And while I didn't think the Court would find me guilty—they might figure out what I was. Doyen would figure it out with her mind reading. I increased the speed of my sawing, no longer trying to be subtle.

I was getting close. *Close.* If I could just finish before they got here...

This moron had set himself up to be caught. But I was a fly who'd gotten stuck in the same web.

"You're a fucking idiot," I said. "One of them can—"

Two figures appeared out of the air. Women. Both statuesque. Both gorgeous and powerful and clearly vampires.

Shit.

They were beautiful and terrifying in the same way that Ares was. I didn't want to look directly at them, or draw attention in any way.

The dark-haired one looked around, her upper lip curled. "This place is disgusting."

"Madam." Aleric stepped forward, then gestured to me. "I present you with Marin Olerafort's murderer. I will accept the bounty at any time."

Ah, a bounty. Smart of the Court. Dumb of Aleric to try to double dip. Getting off the hook *and* getting paid were two things that were too good for the likes of him.

"Madam Magisteria to you." Her voice was cold, her eyes colder.

The other one, Doyen, I assumed, approached us. Her gleaming red hair shined in the light. She was the most beautiful of the two—more beautiful than any woman I'd ever seen—and several of Aleric's goons watched her with slimy eyes.

If I could read their thoughts, I would probably gag.

"This is her?" Doyen's voice was lyrical, her gaze assessing.

I glanced away, sawing frantically at my bonds behind my back. I didn't know how she read minds, but if it was through eye contact, I wouldn't let that happen.

"It is," Aleric said. "I saw her murder him myself."

My head pounded. I shook it, trying to dislodge the invasion. But it did no good.

Shit.

"Get out of my mind," I bit out. Sweat rolled down my back. What was she finding? "Stop it!"

177

The throbbing increased. She was a fucking trespasser.

"Oh!" Her voice sent a shiver through me. "Interesting."

Unable to help myself, I met her gaze. Her blue eyes burned with knowledge, and a little bit of fear.

Shit.

"FireSoul," she whispered.

The earth felt like it fell out from underneath me. My head swam, and my breathing grew quicker.

She knew.

Doyen *knew.* She represented one of the supernatural governments. No way she wouldn't squeal on me to the other two. The Order of the Magica wouldn't hesitate to toss me in the Prison for Magical Miscreants.

I sucked in a ragged breath, pulling myself together. "No idea what you're talking about."

"Hmm." She straightened and turned to Aleric.

No doubt she was giving him the same treatment. Served him right.

I continued to saw at my bonds. Just a little more...

The least thread of my bindings snapped, freeing me. This was it. I had no freaking clue what I was going to do when I got out of here—I was outnumbered, outpowered, and revealed to the Vampire Court—but I'd figure it out.

Twenty feet away from me, Aleric winced. His brow scrunched up.

She was giving him the same crappy head cleaning.

"What are you doing?" he demanded. "What's going on?"

"She can read minds, you moron," I said. "Do your fucking research."

He'd outplayed himself. Too bad I'd gone under the wheels of his runaway bus.

"You're the murderer, Aleric," Doyen said.

And there it was.

"What the hell are you talking about? She did it." Fear flickered in Aleric's eyes. A rat, trapped in a corner. And he was about to bite.

Unfortunately, he had two dozen buddies who would also bite. And I was afraid that the few who were eyeing the beautiful Doyen wanted to do more than bite.

"I hope you've got some fire power up those sleeves of yours, Doyen," I muttered.

She needed to get out more. Didn't she know not to poke a cornered animal?

"You'll come with us, Aleric," she said.

"Ha, lady. I don't think so." Aleric shifted. "I told you that she did it, and I want my money."

"Don't be an idiot. You're the murderer," Doyen said.

"Doyen." Magisteria's voice held a warning note.

Too late.

Aleric's eyes darted. Looking for an escape. When all hell broke lose—that'd be my moment to escape.

The machinery on all sides of the room began to creak and groan, churning to life. Steam poured out of the boilers, beginning to fill the room.

Was this Aleric?

Doors slammed open from behind. Two figures plummeted down from the roof. Ares and a winged demon—Roarke. He was dark gray in his demon form, with massive wings and claws that could tear a head off. Ares, his eyes burning with rage and his fangs fully extended, was just as scary.

A roar sounded from behind me. Aidan's griffin. His footsteps thundered on the ground as he charged. If I had to guess, I'd say he'd broken through the doors using his head as a battering ram.

"Party's over!" Cass shouted from behind me.

"Or starting!" Del yelled.

My heart leapt as chaos erupted. The gang members with magic began firing, shooting fireballs and lightning at my friends.

They attacked back, Ares drawing his shadow sword and Roarke taking to the air.

Aleric turned and ran for it like the coward he so clearly was.

I sliced through the last of my bonds, lunging up. One of Aleric's creepy demon goons grabbed Doyen from behind. She struggled, but couldn't break his hold. The look in his eyes made me queasy. With steam filling the room, it could obscure everything, and he could drag her off somewhere unseen.

I gave one desperate look at Aleric's retreating back, then conjured my bow and arrow and shot Doyen's attacker in the eye. It projected gruesomely from his skull. He collapsed, keeling over like a tree.

She gasped, meeting my gaze.

"Get out of here!" I shouted.

Beside me, Ares stabbed a huge white demon through the gut, spilling his blood on the floor. Aidan, in his massive golden griffin form, chomped his beak around the body of a demon who tried to stab him with a wicked knife. The demon flailed until Aidan bit him in half.

Bile rose in my throat at the sight. In the distance, near where Aleric had run, Cass and Del were surrounded by four demons, but cutting them down quickly. Cass hurled fireballs while Del fought in her Phantom form. She was the only half Phantom in existence, and when she took that form, she was transparent blue. Her blade glowed cobalt, and her translucent hair whipped behind her head.

She was scary as hell. And I liked it.

I raced toward them, hunting Aleric, who'd run past them.

No way I'd let that bastard get away. Marin's killer would not escape. And I *really* wanted to know his secret.

The steam that filled the room made it unbearably warm and difficult to breathe. As I passed Del and Cass, Del lopped the head off their last demon attacker. It thudded to the floor.

"Need help?" Cass yelled.

"Why not!" We were a good team.

I didn't slow, but they joined me, racing toward Aleric's retreating form. Through the steam that filled the room, I could just make out his black-cloaked figure.

He reached the wide metal door at the end of the factory. He slammed into it, trying to push it open. But it held tight.

He backed up and threw out his hands, sending a cloud of black magic toward the door. It collided with the metal, bending it backwards. It wasn't totally destroyed, but it would be with one more blast.

I raised my bow, aiming for his shoulder and hoping I could weaken him enough that he could be apprehended.

I released my arrow, holding my breath as it flew.

As if he heard it whistle through the air, he dodged left at the last moment.

Cass threw a fireball at him. It caught on his cloak, but he shed the flaming garment. Seeming to give up on the door, he glanced toward the ceiling. There was a hole up there, courtesy of my rescuers.

Seeming to make up his mind, he raced for a set of stairs in the corner, about forty meters from the door.

"He's going up!" I called.

I fired one more arrow, but he was too agile. He had some kind of supernatural agility, no question. Even Cass's fireballs missed their mark, and the icicle that Del threw shattered against the wall. Cass and Del had a variety of powers to draw from, each unique. But this guy was too nimble for any of us.

We sprinted after him, cutting through the steam. By the time we reached the stairs leading up to the iron walkway that encircled the whole huge room, he'd reached the top. He turned around and threw out his hands. The stink of his magic welled, making me gag. The same cloud of gray dust burst toward the stairs.

As soon as the magic touched the stairs, they disintegrated.

"Shit, he's a destroyer," I said.

He sprinted down the metal walkway, headed for the next set of stairs.

"I've got this." Cass's magic swelled on the air, the scent of the forest strong. A golden glow shined from her as she transformed into a griffin.

Cass was a Mirror Mage and could mimic the gift of any nearby supernatural. She chose to mimic Aidan, but as usual, her griffin wasn't quite as big or as impressive as his.

She was one of the strongest supernaturals I'd ever met—magic personified—but she hadn't quite gotten the knack for the griffin. Hers was a bit scraggly looking.

But right now, her skinny wings looked pretty good.

I scrambled onto her back, Del behind me. Cass crouched low, then pushed off into the air. I clung to her back as she soared toward the metal walkway, giving Del and me just enough space to climb off.

Aleric was nearly to the next set of stairs, but he turned and blasted his magic behind him. The walkway broke apart, leaving a fifteen-foot gap between us and him.

Too far to jump. What could I conjure to fix this?

Though to be honest, I wasn't sure I had the strength to conjure much of anything. I hadn't had a chance to properly recharge my magic in days, and I was running low.

"Don't worry," Del said.

She stepped forward, extending her hands as her magic swelled around her. Ice shot from her fingertips, forming a bridge where the walkway had disappeared.

She winked at me. "Don't slip."

I grinned and ran across the icy bridge, keeping my hand on the wall for support. By the time I reached the other side, Aleric was almost to the top of the second staircase. I sprinted up after him, my lungs burning. I couldn't give him a chance to blast this thing out from under me.

When he turned to shoot his magic at the stairway, I leapt for him, tossing my bow aside and grasping his ankle. I pulled his legs out from under him, and he crashed hard onto the platform.

"Shouldn't have turned back," I grunted.

He surged upright, sitting and reaching for me. I scrambled up, barely avoiding his grasp. But he wasn't reaching for me. Instead, magic blasted from his fingertips. He aimed for me, but the gray cloud of his destructive magic destroyed the stairs behind me.

Metal creaked and groaned ominously. The struts supporting this part of the platform couldn't hold it.

The walkway beneath us broke away from the wall. We plummeted, hitting the lower platform. Momentum heaved me toward the edge of the platform, but I clambered onto him, avoiding the fifteen-foot plunge to the stone floor below.

He tried to throw me off of him, but I clung hard, conjuring a knife. Aleric grabbed my shoulders and pushed, but he wasn't strong enough to dislodge me. I raised the knife, mind racing. I wanted to immobilize, but not kill.

Though I wanted vengeance for Marin—and this guy was freaking *evil*—I didn't want to kill him if I could help it. He wouldn't get a redo in the Underworld like demons did. I'd rather leave the killing to the Vampire Court if they saw fit.

"Bitch," he rasped.

Changing tactics, he swung his fist at my face. It collided, sending pain through my cheek and making my head spin. All around us, steam filled the room with white clouds. Sweat burned my eyes.

He swung again, and I dodged toward the wall, but the movement made the metal walkaway beneath us creak and groan.

Oh, no.

The metal struts that supported us shrieked as the walkway tore away from the wall and plummeted to the stone floor fifteen feet below. We landed with a crash. I tumbled off of Aleric, my head spinning and breath blown from my lungs.

Ready for another attack, I scrambled for the dagger that I'd dropped and raised it over my head, turning for him.

But his body lay impaled on a piece of metal. One of the iron struts poked right through his chest. Blood soaked his shirt.

My heart lurched.

His gaze was wide and panicked, but he couldn't speak. He had seconds left to live, if that.

"Aleric!"

He said nothing.

I glanced around, but everyone was obscured by the steam. I turned back to Aleric, who was no longer twitching. The life was fading from him quickly.

He was a dead man.

The secrets would die with him.

Unless he'd already told his big boss? He'd been unclear earlier. But what *had* been clear: this secret was a big deal. It would *change everything,* as he'd said.

Shit.

These guys were organized and dedicated. Some kind of crime syndicate or something. And they might have information that could help them immensely. Was I willing to risk letting them have that advantage? I didn't know what their end goal was, but it had to be bad, if a guy as awful as Aleric was excited about it.

And our only lead was inside Aleric's head.

But he was dying. His eyes had gone almost entirely dull.

Shit. I didn't want to do this. Really didn't want to.

I drew in a shuddery breath and reached toward his chest. My hand shook as it neared him, and bile rose in my throat. Around me, the sound of battle prevailed.

I prayed to fate that my friends were safe. Maybe knowing whatever Aleric knew would help with that in the long run.

As soon as my fingertips touched his chest, I gagged. Memories of my time with the Monster rose in my head. I was back there, in his dungeon room, being forced to steal magic to save my mother.

But I'd failed.

I couldn't fail this time.

I breathed shallowly, trying to control my lurching stomach, as I called upon the FireSoul magic within me. I only knew the theory of this, told to me by my mother, but it had to be enough.

I sought the power within me, a banked flame that I'd repressed for decades. It burned low and bright, but I called it forth, fighting the nausea that churned in my stomach.

Worry clouded my mind. Though my mother had said to never use this power, my *deirfiúr* had used theirs and were still good people. I could be too. And we needed to know whatever Aleric knew. It was important. I'd stake my life on it.

The magic swelled within me, a flickering flame that glowed bright purple. It expanded inside my chest, lighting me up with heat as it expanded to my limbs. Purple flames flickered along my arm.

The pain made my eyes tear. It was freaking hot.

The tendrils of fire reached for Aleric, finding his soul and the magic within. It pulled at his two gifts—the Informa magic and the Destroyer magic.

I winced, trying to reject the Destroyer magic. I didn't want that! But it stuck hard to the Informa gift.

In the end, my hesitation didn't matter. The FireSoul magic within me roared, the flame drawing Aleric's power deep inside my chest. I gasped as it filled me, conflicting signatures of darkness and light.

The life faded from Aleric's eyes as I collapsed beside him. My head spun as my soul tried to accommodate the two new magics within me. They were so different—so powerful. The Informa gift was basically knowledge, which was light and good, despite the way it was obtained. But the Destroyer magic... It felt like my chest was full of the same dusty cloud that Aleric had used to destroy the stairs.

The Informa gift bombarded my mind as secrets poured out of it. Most of what I'd taken from Aleric was worthless—secrets of people I didn't know or care about. Betrayals and trickery.

But when his big secret hit me—the information that he'd learned at the Cathar castle—my mind spun. I gasped.

"Dragons," I whispered. "Returned."

CHAPTER FOURTEEN

The rest of the message was confusing, like the Perfecti had said it would be. I couldn't decipher it. But the two words I recognized—those were a big deal. Dragons had been dead for centuries.

But were they not?

Around me, the steam began to dissipate. The battle sounds had decreased as well.

I struggled to my feet, stomach lurching.

Had I made a terrible mistake?

Very possibly.

But what I'd learned...

I searched for my friends. Cass and Del were running toward me through the dissipating steam. Ares finished off the last demon, while Roarke and Aidan prowled the perimeter. Bodies were scattered throughout the warehouse, most disappearing because they were demons. In the corner, Magisteria and Doyen stood. Magisteria held a blade coated with blood. The body of a demon lay crumpled in front of them.

"Nix!" Cass skidded to a stop in front of me. "Are you all right?"

"Fine." I drew in a ragged breath. "Just fine."

"Really?" Del searched my face.

"We can talk about it later."

Behind their backs, Magisteria and Doyen were approaching. Ares, who'd just cut the head off the last demon, noticed. He joined them.

The three of them walking toward me in a line made my knees shake.

Aidan and Roarke loped up to join us, skirting around the trio of vampires and standing next to Del and Cass. All four turned to stand between me and the vampires.

Their support made tears prickle at the corners of my eyes. But I couldn't let them stand between me and danger. Especially when Del and Cass were FireSouls too. But their secret was still safe.

I nudged them aside and stepped between my friends and the vampires.

When Cass hissed in my ear, I ignored her. Magisteria and Doyen's faces were expressionless. And whatever was on Ares's face, I couldn't read it. Maybe I didn't want to read it.

Could they tell that I'd just used my FireSoul power? They hadn't seen me through the steam, and I didn't think I looked any different.

Magisteria glanced past me toward the body of Aleric. "He is dead?"

I nodded. "He is."

"Good. No more than he deserved." Her gaze fell to the collar at my neck. "We will remove that."

My breath caught. That was a good sign. They'd probably want to keep it on if they were going to try to turn me in to the Order of the Magica.

"Okay." I waited, tense as a board, while each of the vampires touched their fingertips to the collar. It heated briefly, then fell away.

My chest felt like it opened up—like I could breathe for the first time in three days. Thank fates.

"As for the other," Doyen said. "We will consult and be in touch."

"Other what?" Cass asked.

"Um— It's nothing. I'll tell you later." Shit. What should I do? If I let them walk out of here with knowledge of what I was…

My life could be over.

My friends and I technically had the magical firepower to stop them—but there was only one way to do it. And it'd make us murderers. I couldn't ask them for that. Especially since Ares was so strong that we might not all make it out alive.

I met Ares's gaze. Did he know?

His brow furrowed as he glanced at Doyen. He didn't.

It was settled.

If I had to run for it, I would. Because I wasn't about to start a fight that would risk my friends' lives just to save my own hide. No way I could live with myself if I did that.

"We should go," I said to my friends. "Especially since whoever is in charge of these goons might realize we've just killed a bunch of his henchmen."

"All right." Cass glared at the vampires.

I didn't blame her. They were pretty unlikable. All except Ares, who I still didn't know what to make of.

"We will be in touch," Magisteria said.

I nodded, then turned. The back of my neck tingled as I walked away. They were definitely watching us. My friends and I left the old factory and went into the cold, dark night. We were on the far side of our neighborhood, about a half mile from our street.

"I can't believe this happened so close to our homes," I said.

"There's a first for everything," Cass said.

"What was that weirdness all about?" Del asked.

"I'll tell you when we get home." I walked briskly, ready to get behind the safety of my locked doors. The memory of the silver sonic bomb flashed in my mind. "What happened after I was abducted?"

"We heard the blast," Nix said. "Just a boom. Like a sonic bomb."

"Yeah, that's what it was." I turned left down our street.

"We ran outside," Cass said. "By the time we made it down the street, you'd been dragged off. Ares was fighting three guys, but he had a concussion and wasn't doing too well."

"Really?"

"Well, he still killed them all," Aidan said. "But after seeing him tonight, I realize he could have done it in a fraction of the time."

"Yeah, he's not bad in a fight." Being a mixed vampire mage hybrid would do that for a guy.

"It took us an hour to find you," Del said. "We used our dragon senses to track you, but it was tricky. I think they had some kind of concealment charm on you. Not a strong one, but enough to delay us a bit."

"Yeah." I held up my wrist and removed the brass bangle. In the heat of the moment, I'd forgotten the bracelet. "Thanks for finding me, though."

"Anytime. What went on back there?" Cass asked as we reached our green door.

"Let's chat in my place, okay?" I asked.

"Sure. Girls only?" Del asked.

I looked at Aidan and Roarke. We were friends—family, even —but right now... Right now I wanted only my deirfiúr. "Yeah, if that's okay."

"No problem." Aidan grinned. "Glad you're better."

"Seconded," Roarke said.

"Thanks, guys." We left them, heading up to my apartment.

They took a seat on the couch while I scavenged in the fridge and came up with three of Cass's PBRs that she'd stashed there a while ago. I really needed to get to the store.

I returned to the living room and held them up. "Who wants a drink?"

"That's all you've got?" Del asked.

"Yep. And you're going to like it," I said.

"I'm going to tolerate it." Del took a can and popped it open.

Cass followed suit, sighing contentedly. I collapsed on the couch, my muscles melting into the cushions. I opened my own beer and took a big swig. "I did it. I used my FireSoul gift."

Both gasped.

"Really?" Cass asked. "I thought it made you sick."

"Still does." Even now, my stomach was feeling woozy. Not to mention the weird magic now camped out in my chest and the prophecy floating around in my head. At least, I was pretty sure the secret was a prophecy.

"Why now?" Del asked. "Was it to steal his Informa power? To get that secret?"

"Yeah. It felt necessary. I don't think this thing with the dragon tattoo gang is over. There's more to it than we realized, and that secret is part of it."

"What was it?" Cass asked.

I met her gaze, confusion racing around inside my head. "I think so. I only understood two words, which is what the Cathar Perfecti said would happen. That I wouldn't be able to understand it all because of how they encode the information."

"What are the words?" Del asked.

"Dragons. And return."

Cass's eyes widened, and Del's jaw slackened.

"What?" Del said.

"Dragons are dead," Cass added.

"Yeah. I think it's a prophecy. It's the secret Aleric was getting for his Master, the person who must be in charge of all those dragon tattoo minions."

"They're dead though. And most were demons anyway. Hired mercs." Del sipped her beer, her expression thoughtful.

"There will be more where they came from, though. They're dedicated." The memory of the two who committed suicide flashed in my mind. I shivered. That kind of dedication...

Cultlike.

"So we need to figure out what this prophecy is," Del said. "Do you think he told his Master?"

"I don't know. But the prophecy is important, whatever it is."

"That's one important loose thread," Cass said. "We'll have to figure this out."

"Agreed." Dragons whispered in my head over and over. So did the idea of some shady bossman calling the shots with a bunch of evil minions.

"I also got his Destroyer magic." I drew in a ragged breath. My queasy stomach was not making this easy. "But it feels like crap. I think it's making me ill."

"No good without the bad," Cass said. "But you can learn to control it."

"I hope so. Because it feels terrible."

"You'll learn," Del said. "Taking powers requires that you learn. Your skills will grow, but you have to control them or they'll overtake you."

The queasiness confirmed her statement. This was gross. A polluting magic that I'd need to master so that it didn't incapacitate me.

"And there's one more thing. It's worse," I said.

"Yeah?" Del asked.

"Doyen, one of the vampires, read my mind. She knows I'm a FireSoul."

Cass and Del gasped.

"Shit," Cass said.

"Not good," Del added.

"I think I need to run for it. Lie low for a little while. They can't come back around here—especially not Doyen. She could read your minds too."

"You can't run," Cass said.

"Not far. Not forever." But even the idea made my head ache. I didn't want to run. I hadn't been parted from them since the moment we woke in the field at fifteen.

"I don't know. There's got to be something we can do," Del said.

"Kill them," Cass said.

"No!" I squeezed her hand. "We can't."

"To protect you, I could." Her voice was fierce.

"Thanks." I smiled weakly. "I appreciate it. But I don't think killing them all is the answer. I just don't know what is."

"We'll think of—"

Something clattered against the window at the front of my apartment. I looked up. A small pebble hit the glass. Then another.

"You may have a visitor," Cass said.

I got up and walked to the window, then peered out. Ares stood below. I pushed open the window, my skin chilled before the cold night air rushed in. He knew what I was now. Doyen would have told him.

Most thought we were evil.

What would he think?

Given what his mother had done for a living, I was pretty sure I knew.

"What do you want?" I called down.

"To talk to you."

I turned back to my friends. "What do you think?"

"Might as well talk to him," Cass said. "He might be on your side."

"I doubt it."

"Only one way to know," Del said. "Talk to him."

I turned back to the window. "You aren't going to try to transport me away from here, right?"

That was the last thing I needed.

"I won't. On my honor."

I studied his eyes. I trusted him. I didn't know what he was going to say, but he wouldn't try to forcibly remove me from here. I wouldn't let him.

"Fine," I called. "I'll be right down."

I turned back to my friends. "You guys can go."

"You sure?" Del asked.

"Yeah. I've got this. Once I hear what he has to say, we'll come up with a plan. If it's leaving, then it's leaving." Though my heart ached to think of it.

"Fine." Cass hugged me, then left. Del did the same.

I watched them head up the stairs to their places, then I walked down to the main door. I pulled it open to find Ares on the step. I held out my hand. "Stop right there."

"I know what you are."

"I figured." I searched his eyes, but they were unreadable. "And?"

"I don't care."

"What? Uh, what about your mother? Wasn't she head of the committee to hunt FireSouls?"

"That was a long time ago." He frowned. "When I was younger, I agreed with her zealousness. She was my mother. And I'll admit I've been wary of FireSouls my entire life. But you're different."

Annoyance filled my chest. "No, I'm not. I've met other Fire-Souls who live in their own realm, and they aren't evil." I was careful to say how they lived far away, in their own realm. I didn't trust him enough to point him toward Del or Cass. "They're good people. Just because we can do bad by stealing powers didn't mean that we do. FireSouls have been getting a bad rap for centuries."

I'd done it tonight, but only once the guy was already dying and because I hoped it would lead to the greater good. I didn't like myself for it, because it still felt kinda self-serving, but I'd been trying to be good.

"They get a bad rap from people who are frightened," he said. "But I'm not scared of anything. And I could tell if you're evil. It's my job. You're far from evil, Nix."

Hmm. A flicker of optimism lit in my chest. "This is surprising. Everyone thinks FireSouls are evil. You don't?"

He shook his head. "You're smart, tough, and you have a moral compass set to dead center."

"Oh." I hadn't expected compliments.

"And I like you, Nix. A lot."

Surprise flared in my chest. He stepped forward, putting his hand on my waist. I stiffened, but didn't shove him away.

It felt nice. More than nice.

"And I want to spend more time with you." He leaned down, his green eyes intent on mine.

"You do?" I stared at his lips, unable to look away. Tension fizzed in the air between us. He tugged me slightly closer. My breath caught. He was going to kiss me.

Instead of letting him make the first move, I stood on my tiptoes and threw my arms around his neck, pressing my lips to his. He groaned and pulled me closer, parting my lips with his tongue and kissing me until I saw stars.

Finally, I gasped and pulled away. I stepped back and put up a hand. "Don't think that means anything. I just wanted to get that out of my system."

"And?"

"Not bad." More than not bad. It was great. My head was still spinning. "So the Vampire Court is fine with me?"

I grinned, hardly able to believe that I was off the hook.

Ares frowned. "Well, no."

I stepped back, startled. "Wait, what? They aren't? You tell me this after you kiss me?"

"Technically, you kissed me first."

I scowled. "My mistake. I thought everything was good. You just said you didn't think I was evil."

"I don't. But Magisteria and Doyen are suspicious. They wanted to turn you over to the Order of the Magica, but I've convinced them to hold onto the information and give you a chance."

My head pounded. "So you ordered them not to tell the Magica?"

Was I at least safe from that, for now?

"I did. But it will not last. It's not just that you are a FireSoul that makes them wary—you can walk in the Shadowlands. You shouldn't be able to do that. You aren't a Vampire or one of our allies. Only powerful dark magic could permit you to walk there. Like the kind that Aleric used to allow him to stalk Marin before he killed him."

"I didn't use dark magic. You're nuts. I have no idea why I can walk there."

"And that's what has Magisteria and Doyen so wary. Myself as well. You possess strange magic, Nix. It makes you dangerous. The Vampire Court has demanded that you complete a series of trials and an interview to prove you're an ally. That we can trust you."

"Hell, no."

"They will turn you over. And your friends, for harboring you."

I shoved him. "No! I helped you with this case. You can't do this to me now."

"You'll be fine. You'll complete the challenges and prove you're trustworthy. Then your secret will be safe. Better yet, you'll have Vampire protection."

That piqued my interest. "Really? That means you'd defend me. Hunt anyone who hurt me. Like you did with Marin."

"It's a two way street, Nix. If you can earn their trust—my trust—it will help you."

"What about my trust?" I asked.

"I'll try to earn that too." His gaze was serious.

"And my alternative is them turning me and my friends in to the Order?" I gnawed on my lower lip.

"Yes. And we won't put a collar on you. Not like last time. You must complete the trials of your own volition. But I'll help you."

"I don't need your help." I didn't want his help. Maybe this was his idea of a favor—him convincing the rest of the Court to let me audition to be an ally. But it felt pretty shitty right now.

"You'll need it."

I could just run. But I didn't want to. And I wouldn't. I'd spend too much of my life running. And he said that they'd turn in my friends for harboring a FireSoul. I couldn't let that happen. Especially when they were FireSouls. They'd be found out.

"Fine. I'll do it. Whatever their dumb challenges are—I'll beat them." I poked him hard in the chest. "But forget that kiss. We're all business from here on out. Nothing funny."

"Oh, I promise you won't be laughing."

I grinned, then frowned. I needed to keep a straight head where he was concerned. "Whatever. I'm going to focus on these challenges."

"We'll both focus on them."

I frowned at him. "Apparently so."

I was still wary of him and my trust wasn't at one hundred percent. But if I'd learned anything in my time as a FireSoul, you were always stronger in numbers. And I had a feeling I was going to need every advantage I could get. With the new magic roiling around in my system and the Vampire Court breathing down my neck, I'd need all the help I could get.

THANK YOU FOR READING!

I hope you enjoyed reading this book as much as I enjoyed writing it. Reviews are *so* helpful to authors. I really appreciate all reviews, both positive and negative. If you want to leave one, you can do so at Amazon or GoodReads.

AUTHOR'S NOTE

Thank you so much for reading *Fugitive of Magic*! As with all of my books, I included historical and mythological elements. If you're interested in reading more about that, read on. At the end, I'll talk a bit about why Nix and her *deirfiúr* are treasure hunters and how I try to make that fit with archaeology's ethics (which don't condone treasure hunting, as I'm sure you might have guessed).

Now, onto the history in *Fugitive of Magic*! The artifacts that Nix and her *deirfiúr* collect and preserve come from all different cultures and periods. The clay vase that the demons were attempting to steal was from the Bell Beaker culture, which lasted from approximately 2900 - 1800 BC. It spread across western Europe and was characterized by distinctive bell-shaped pottery vessels that were used for everything from drinking to funerary urns. It was the first instance of cultural contact on such a massive scale—they have been found in areas stretching as far as Scotland to southern Italy and eastern Europe.

The rest of the historical elements to the book are slightly more modern. Saint Pancras station, which houses the Order of the Secret Stealers, is a magnificent Victorian building built in the 1860s. To my knowledge, there are no underground Roman warehouses (called horrea) or shops underneath Saint Pancras station, but they do exist in Narbonne France. If the Romans built them at that side of their empire, perhaps they built them in London, which they called Londinium.

The last bit of history that I included are the Cathar castles in southern France. The Cathars were a religious sect founded in the 11th century AD. They were supported by the local people and lords, some of whom were Cathars themselves. They built incredible castles at the peaks of mountains across the Languedoc region. The Catholic Church waged a Crusade against the Cathars in the thirteenth century. Many of the battles were conducted at the Cathar castles. Though their mountaintop castles were impressive, they were not enough to protect the from the Crusade. Nearly all Cathars were killed during the Medieval period, but their strongholds still stand.

That's it for the historical influences in *Fugitive of Magic*. However, one of the most important things about this book is how Nix and her *deirfiúr* treat artifacts and their business, Ancient Magic.

As I'm sure you know, archaeology isn't quite like Indiana Jones (for which I'm both grateful and bitterly disappointed). Sure, it's exciting and full of travel. However, booby-traps are not as common as I expected. Total number of booby-traps I have encountered in my career: zero. Still hoping, though.

When I chose to write a series about archaeology and treasure hunting, I knew I had a careful line to tread. There is a big difference between these two activities. As much as I value artifacts, they are not treasure. Not even the gold artifacts. They are pieces of our history that contain valuable information, and as such, they belong to all of us. Every artifact that is excavated should be properly conserved and stored in a museum so that everyone can have access to our history. No one single person can own history, and I believe very strongly that individuals should not own artifacts. Treasure hunting is the pursuit of artifacts for personal gain.

So why did I make Nix and her *deirfiúr* treasure hunters? I'd have loved to call them archaeologists, but nothing about their work is like archaeology. Archaeology is a very laborious, painstaking process—and it certainly doesn't involve selling artifacts. That wouldn't work for the fast-paced, adventurous series that I had planned for *Dragon's Gift*. Not to mention the fact that dragons are famous for coveting treasure. Considering where the *deirfiúr* got their skills from, it just made sense to call them treasure hunters.

Even though I write urban fantasy, I strive for accuracy. The *deirfiúr* don't engage in archaeological practices—therefore, I cannot call them archaeologists. I also have a duty as an archaeologist to properly represent my field and our goals—namely, to protect and share history. Treasure hunting doesn't do this. One of the biggest battles that archaeology faces today is protecting cultural heritage from thieves.

I debated long and hard about not only what to call the heroines of this series, but also about how they would do their jobs. I wanted it to involve all the cool things we think about when we think about archaeology—namely, the Indiana Jones stuff, whether it's real or not. But I didn't know quite how to do that while still staying within the bounds of my own ethics. I can cut myself and other writers some slack because this is fiction, but I couldn't go too far into smash and grab treasure hunting.

I consulted some of my archaeology colleagues to get their take, which was immensely helpful. Wayne Lusardi, the State Maritime Archaeologist for Michigan, and Douglas Inglis and Veronica Morris, both archaeologists for Interactive Heritage, were immensely helpful with ideas. My biggest problem was figuring out how to have the heroines steal artifacts from tombs and then sell them and still sleep at night. Everything I've just said is pretty counter to this, right?

That's where the magic comes in. The heroines aren't after the artifacts themselves (they put them back where they found them, if you recall)—they're after the magic that the artifacts contain. They're more like magic hunters than treasure hunters. That solved a big part of my problem. At least they were putting the artifacts back. Though that's not proper archaeology, I could let it pass. At least it's clear that they believe they shouldn't keep the artifact or harm the site. But the SuperNerd in me said, "Well, that magic is part of the artifact's context. It's important to the artifact and shouldn't be removed and sold."

Now *that* was a problem. I couldn't escape my SuperNerd self, so I was in a real conundrum. Fortunately, that's where the immensely intelligent Wayne Lusardi came in. He suggested that the magic could have an expiration date. If the magic wasn't used before it decayed, it could cause huge problems. Think explosions and tornado spells run amok. It could ruin the entire site, not to mention possibly cause injury and death. That would be very bad.

So now you see why Nix and her *deirfiúr* don't just steal artifacts to sell them. Not only is selling the magic cooler, it's also better from an ethical standpoint, especially if the magic was going to cause problems in the long run. These aren't perfect solutions—the perfect solution would be sending in a team of archaeologists to carefully record the site and remove the dangerous magic—but that wouldn't be a very fun book.

Thanks again for reading (especially if you got this far!). I hope you enjoyed the story and will stick with Nix on the rest of her adventure!

GLOSSARY

Alpha Council - There are two governments that enforce law for supernaturals—the Alpha Council and the Order of the Magica. The Alpha Council governs all shifters. They work cooperatively with the Alpha Council when necessary—for example, when capturing FireSouls.

Blood Sorceress - A type of Magica who can create magic using blood.

Conjurer - A Magica who uses magic to create something from nothing. They cannot create magic, but if there is magic around them, they can put that magic into their conjuration.

Dark Magic - The kind that is meant to harm. It's not necessarily bad, but it often is.

Deirfiúr - Sisters in Irish.

Demons - Often employed to do evil. They live in various hells but can be released upon the earth if you know how to get to them and then get them out. If they are killed on Earth, they are sent back to their hell.

Dragon Sense - A FireSoul's ability to find treasure. It is an internal sense that pulls them toward what they seek. It is easiest to find gold, but they can find anything or anyone that is valued by someone.

Elemental Mage – A rare type of mage who can manipulate all of the elements.

Enchanted Artifacts – Artifacts can be imbued with magic that lasts after the death of the person who put the magic into the artifact (unlike a spell that has not been put into an artifact—these spells disappear after the Magica's death). But magic is not stable. After a period of time—hundreds or thousands of years depending on the circumstance—the magic will degrade. Eventually, it can go bad and cause many problems.

Fire Mage – A mage who can control fire.

FireSoul - A very rare type of Magica who shares a piece of the dragon's soul. They can locate treasure and steal the gifts (powers) of other supernaturals. With practice, they can manipulate the gifts they steal, becoming the strongest of that gift. They are despised and feared. If they are caught, they are thrown in the Prison of Magical Deviants.

The Great Peace - The most powerful piece of magic ever created. It hides magic from the eyes of humans.

Hearth Witch – A Magica who is versed in magic relating to hearth and home. They are often good at potions and protective spells and are also very perceptive when on their own turf.

Informa - A supernatural who can steal powers.

Magica - Any supernatural who has the power to create magic —witches, sorcerers, mages. All are governed by the Order of the Magica.

The Origin - The descendent of the original alpha shifter. They are the most powerful shifter and can turn into any species.

Order of the Magica - There are two governments that enforce law for supernaturals—the Alpha Council and the Order of the Magica. The Order of the Magica govern all Magica. They work cooperatively with the Alpha Council when necessary—for example, when capturing FireSouls.

Phantom - A type of supernatural that is similar to a ghost. They are incorporeal. They feed off the misery and pain of others, forcing them to relive their greatest nightmares and fears. They do not have a fully functioning mind like a human or supernatural. Rather, they are a shadow of their former selves. Half-bloods are extraordinarily rare.

Seeker - A type of supernatural who can find things. FireSouls often pass off their dragon sense as Seeker power.

Shifter - A supernatural who can turn into an animal. All are governed by the Alpha Council.

Transporter - A type of supernatural who can travel anywhere. Their power is limited and must regenerate after each use.

Vampire - Blood drinking supernaturals with great strength and speed who live in a separate realm.

Warden of the Underworld - A one of a kind position created by Roarke. He keeps order in the Underworld.

ABOUT LINSEY

Before becoming a writer, Linsey Hall was a nautical archaeologist who studied shipwrecks from Hawaii and the Yukon to the UK and the Mediterranean. She credits fantasy and historical romances with her love of history and her career as an archaeologist. After a decade of tromping around the globe in search of old bits of stuff that people left lying about, she settled down and started penning her own romance novels. Her Dragon's Gift series draws upon her love of history and the paranormal elements that she can't help but include.

COPYRIGHT

Made in the USA
Lexington, KY
06 July 2017